W9-DIE-714

THE WIZARD OF DEATH

A NOVEL OF SUSPENSE

RICHARD FORREST

The Bobbs-Merrill Company, Inc.
Indianapolis/New York

Also by Richard Forrest:

A Child's Garden of Death
Who Killed Mr. Garland's Mistress?

Published by the Bobbs-Merrill Company, Inc.
Indianapolis New York

Designed by Lou Keach

Manufactured in the United States of America

First printing

Library of Congress Cataloging in Publication Data

Forrest, Richard, 1932-
The wizard of death.

I. Title.
PZ4.F72887Wi [PS3556.0739] 813'.5'4 76-46226
ISBN 0-672-52238-1

In memory of

David R. Storey

1

Gerbils and gophers . . . Yes, *The Gopher on the Green* might work.

A political rally had replaced long-ago musters of militia on the town green as Lyon Wentworth sat on a warm car fender and wondered if *The Gopher on the Green* would be a workable title for his next children's book. He let his mind wander and paid scant attention to the speaker's platform near the Civil War monument.

He frowned as a red balloon began a rapid ascent toward the clear July sky.

He pushed himself off the fender and took three steps to reach its trailing string before realizing it was too late. It was at treetop level when its three-year-old owner discovered her loss. A small cry of anguish merged into the drone from the platform.

He knelt on one knee beside the small girl, and together they watched the helium-filled balloon disappear over the church steeple.

"It's gone where happy balloons go," he said.

"Where?"

"To Emerald City to stay with the Wizard of Oz, of course."

"Oh." She looked at him with wide brown eyes until a tentative smile emerged. She looked up for the last time at the departed balloon, waved, and ran across the grass toward her mother.

Lyon turned to look beyond the rows of people sitting on blankets and folding chairs before the temporary platform to see that his wife was now speaking from the podium.

Bea Wentworth, her figure trim and well proportioned, spoke with an energy that seemed to possess her slight body. Occasionally, as if to emphasize a point, her hand would ruffle the edge of her closely cropped hair.

". . . a fine lawyer, a dedicated family man, the next nominee of our party and the next governor of our state, Randolph Llewyn!"

As she concluded, her voice rose and reverberated from the several amplifiers placed around the Murphysville Town Green. Bea turned quickly from the podium as the angular man seated at her side rose and shook hands.

Randolph Llewyn raised both arms over his head in acknowledgment of the rising applause—and fell dead as a rifle cracked twice.

A gasp issued from the crowd. At the corner of the green Lyon instinctively crouched by a car fender. On the speaker's platform the frozen tableau began to react in short, jerky motions. Bea knelt next to the fallen candidate, while the others flung themselves behind the scant protection of folding chairs. Rocco Herbert, the town's chief of police, was on one knee in front of the platform, his left hand steadying the right as he aimed a Magnum revolver.

The large police officer spaced carefully aimed shots at two-second intervals. The thunder of the powerful handgun was picked up by the stage microphone and echoed across the confused green.

Lyon visually followed the chief's 60-degree angle of aim and saw wood splintering around the edges of a small belfry window two-thirds of the way up the church steeple.

Two more and the gun would be empty.

Lyon sprinted toward the nearby squad car and fumbled over the visor for the ignition keys he knew the chief kept there. He had the car moving as Rocco Herbert loped across the grass toward him. Reaching across the seat, Lyon opened the far car door and Rocco flung himself inside. The car accelerated as the chief spilled spent shells over his lap and frantically began to reload the weapon.

"Back of the goddamned church!" Rocco yelled.

Lyon careened the car across the lawn of Amsten House (built 1732) next to the Congregational Church, jumped the curb of the church drive and skidded into the parking lot. Thirty yards away a trail bike, its marker plate obscured by mud, was weaving back and forth between the ancient gravestones of the colonial cemetery at the rear of the church.

"The lane!" Rocco yelled.

"What lane?"

"To the right, damn it!"

Lyon swerved the wheel, throwing the car into a skidding turn inches from the cemetery's wrought-iron fence, and turned toward the right, where a small lane ran along the sides of the graves. The motorcyclist had to weave around the headstones, which allowed the car to close the gap. The two vehicles were almost parallel when the trail bike took a tangent toward an open iron gate and sped through onto the rear meadow.

A barbed-wire fence blocked the end of the lane, and Lyon took his foot off the accelerator and frantically braked the rocking car. Rocco's size 14-D shoe knocked Lyon's foot off the brake and then slammed down on the gas. The car jumped ahead and smashed through the fence. A twanging piece of wire snapped through the open window and tore a small gash along Lyon's arm as Rocco leaned out the other window and tried to aim the revolver as the car jounced over the pasture.

As they raced along the incline of the meadow, a few cud-chewing cows looked at the two speeding vehicles with complete uninterest. Small scrub pines snapped against the car as it labored along the path of the trail bike. The angle of the hill increased; glacial boulders strewn over the path before them narrowed possible clearance for the car.

Rocco fired a wild shot from the swaying vehicle and then yelled at Lyon, "The boulders ahead, we'll never—"

The car attempted passage between two large rock formations; metal tore, and strange grinding noises came from the undercarriage as Lyon tried to brake to a halt. The car stopped with a jolt that threw both men against the dashboard.

"—make it," Rocco said tiredly as he held a

handkerchief against his bleeding nose. Both men were quiet as the whine of the trail bike retreated into the distance.

"I'd like to see about my wife," Lyon said as Rocco reached for the radio transmitter and began to give curt instructions.

Lyon Wentworth stood in the bedroom doorway with two thimbles of slightly warmed Dry Sack sherry. The small figure curled in a ball on the large bed with a sheet pulled tight at the neck seemed childlike, a person bundling away from the monsters of life.

He put the sherry on the night table and sat on the edge of the bed and gently caressed her head. Bea snuffled and pressed her nose deeper into the pillow. We're all so basically vulnerable, Lyon thought. He knew his wife had a legion of male and female admirers throughout the state. State Senator Beatrice Wentworth, a feisty member of the legislature who strode through the Victorian halls of the state capitol intent on jousting with her myriad foes . . . attack when necessary and fear not. At times she had joined battle with governors and congressmen and recently had decimated a presidential cabinet member on a local interview show . . . now she lay curled in the fetal position.

He bent over and kissed the nape of her neck. He wanted to lie next to her and fold her in his arms, but the secret warning bell formed over years of marriage told him that he should wait.

Bea gave a deep moan, turned over and abruptly sat up. Tears crossed her cheeks.

"GOD DAMN IT, WENTWORTH! WHY DO THEY ALWAYS KILL THE GOOD GUYS?"

6

He held her against his shoulder. "I don't know," he whispered.

She wiped her eyes with the edge of the sheet and bolted from the bed. Her small fists came down with a thud on the dresser top. "IT'S GOT TO STOP!"

Lyon picked up the minute hearing aid from the night table, flipped it on and inserted it in her ear. He handed her the sherry, which she drained in one gulp. "It's probably a nut; political assassins usually are."

"He was a good man, Lyon. A fine legislator, an honest man who could have done a hell of a lot for this state. Maybe more, he would have eventually gone on. . . I don't know how far he might have gone, and all of it would have been good."

"Would you like me to have the doctor give you a sedative?"

"I don't want a pill. I'm too mad for a sedative!"

"There's nothing you can do about it, Bea."

"Like hell there isn't!"

He saw in her eyes that tears had been replaced by an angry glint. "What do you have in mind?" Lyon asked softly.

"Guns, damn it!"

"It's hardly your style to take to the streets."

"Not that. I'm going to see that they're taken away from the idiots."

"That doesn't sound like Bea Wentworth, champion of civil liberties."

"Free speech isn't the right for any idiot to carry a lethal weapon. Anyone able to stumble into a sporting-goods store can buy almost any type of rifle he wants."

"Some people hunt."

"Rifles aren't legal to hunt with in this state—only shotguns. He fired from the church steeple, didn't he?"

"Yes. We found him in back of the church where we chased him."

"That's what?—maybe two hundred yards from the speaker's platform."

"More or less."

"Well, he sure as hell couldn't have done it with a shotgun."

"Try to get some sleep, Bea. There's nothing we can do about it tonight."

Her voice dropped and her eyes clouded. "When I got home after it happened, I found blood on my clothes. Part of Randy Llewyn's brains were on my blouse . . . the life force of a good man was—was . . ." She turned away to stare out the window. "I can do something about it. It's about time this state had some decent gun legislation."

"You're bucking powerful forces. More guns are manufactured in Connecticut than in the rest of the states put together."

"Then it's about time they made yo-yos or teddy bears." She strode to her desk in the corner of the room and snatched up a pen and clipboard. Returning to the bed, she fluffed a pillow, sat up against the headboard and furiously began to make notes. She paused for a moment and looked past Lyon. "If I make a trade-off with my vote against the highway bill with Senator Marcuse, he might back a gun-legislation bill. Jenkins is a Quaker; he'll co-sponsor. But I need Williams on my welfare reform bill . . ." She continued staring into space and chewing the end of her pen.

Lyon shrugged and started from the room. "I think I'll see if I can get some work done." He softly closed the door.

"WENTWORTH, GET BACK HERE!"

Lyon opened the door again and stuck his

head back into the bedroom. "You screamed, dear?"

"Don't get any ideas."

"What do you mean?"

"You know damn well what I mean. I mean no ideas between you and your friend, big chief. This is Murphysville's first murder in a long time, and it's a job for the state police. If you want to do something, you can help me by writing news articles and other PR stuff advocating gun legislation."

"Thank you for my instructions." Lyon smiled as Bea went back to her notes.

He walked slowly through the darkened house, trying not to think about Randy Llewyn's death.

Lyon Wentworth was a tall man who usually wore tennis sneakers without socks, denim pants and light sport shirts. His deep-cut facial lines often gave him a faraway and troubled look, but when he pushed back a forelock of blond-browning hair and smiled, he transformed that look to a fey expression of warmth.

In his study he slid into the chair before the desk. The lamp cast a glow on the unfinished manuscript to the right of the typewriter. He leafed through the pages. The book, *The Wobblies Strike Again*, was only a third completed, and so far the Wobblies hadn't struck very far. The Wobblies were benign monsters, and the children's book series concerning them had been his most successful, so successful that a national toy maker had created Wobbly dolls, two of which reposed on the study's mantel. He tried to make his pleasant monsters encompass all childhood fears and reduce them to manageable proportions.

He wondered if perhaps he hadn't been wrong over the years. Perhaps it wasn't things that go bump in the night or creatures that hovered in the dark that were the inchoate fears of life—possibly it was a strange fate, kismet, or luck that the gods called down upon us. Randy Llewyn, for all his attributes as a man and candidate, had by a stroke of ill luck set off a maniacal element in some crazed mind; if he hadn't, he would be here now, having cocktails and steaks at Nutmeg Hill House with Bea and others.

When the phone rang he glared at it. He had always thought that telephones were the devil's gift to mankind, along with such other devious devices as political campaigns, the internal-combustion engine, and hips on certain women you aren't married to. He reached for the ominous device, held it several inches from his ear, and uttered a tentative "Hello."

"That you, Wentworth? Colonel Thornburton here."

Oh, Jesus. It was Stacey Thornburton, his illustrator. The reversion to his former military title was a sure indication that something was amiss. "Hi, Stacey. How's the weather down there?"

"Passable, Wentworth, barely passable. Something has come up that will affect our relationship. I've got to reorient my priorities, and drawing pictures for kids is out."

"What's the matter? Don't you like the outline for the new book?"

"The outline's fine. It's my kid—Robin. We have a real crisis down here. Robin refuses to go to West Point."

"I'm sorry to hear that, but there are a lot of other good schools around."

"Not with true military tradition, Wentworth. I might accept the Citadel, or, in a pinch, V.M.I., but it would never be the same—those Saturdays on the parade ground, plebe hazing—nothing like it."

"What college does Robin have in mind?"

"Bard or Antioch. You won't believe this, Wentworth, it's hard to imagine, but those schools don't even have ROTC."

"Have you done any work at all on *The Wobblies Strike Again?*"

"No. That's why I'm on the horn. I'm sending the outline back. I have retired from the artistic world."

"You don't want to do that, Stacey."

"How do you expect me to raise a child with guts when daddy spends all day drawing pictures for children's books?"

"You had a fine military record, Colonel," Lyon replied respectfully, although he knew Stacey Thornburton, Colonel, U.S.A., Retired, had spent twenty years in the Quartermaster Corps.

"Robin forgets all that, Lyon."

"Let Robin make the choice."

"She doesn't know her own mind."

"I don't know about North Carolina, but here in Connecticut there are a lot of girls who don't want to go to West Point."

"Four great years of drill and discipline; she doesn't know what she's missing."

"Sleep on it, Stacey," Lyon said and hung up. Stacey and Lyon had met eight years earlier in a New York publisher's office. Lyon's first book had been purchased; and Stacey's, entitled, *Army Brat*, had been turned down, although there were many compliments on his fey illustrations. Lyon's editor had suggested that they consider a collaboration.

Lyon and the colonel had adjourned to a nearby cocktail lounge. After an hour's harangue on military tactics in Korea, Lyon had dismissed any possibility of collaborating with the former military officer.

Lyon wasn't sure when it happened, but he

thought it fell somewhere between a critique of Monty's tactics at El Alamein and MacArthur's at the Inchon Reservoir when Stacey had begun to sketch on a small pad. With deft strokes, he quickly finished the ink drawing and gave it to Lyon.

"I think your characters, the Wobblies, look like this," Stacey had said in an embarrassed aside.

Lyon had been stunned. With a few lines the colonel had created a drawing that brought the Wobblies to life. Lyon's benign monsters stared from the paper with the exact qualities he had always imagined they possessed. From that point on, there had never been any doubt that they would continue as a team.

For a moment he speculated on his two uniformed friends: one, a retired military officer who approached a near caricature of his breed; and the other, a police chief whose massive appearance seemed to categorize the man. And yet, in each man a deep vein of gentleness, often hidden from the exterior world, was the very essence of his being. In that, there might be hope for us all.

The phone rang again, and he snatched it up in irritation. "Go to sleep, Stacey. I'll call you in the morning."

"I've got something on the Llewyn killing," Rocco Herbert's voice said without preamble.

"I'm not home," Lyon said and stuffed the phone into the bottom desk drawer and covered it with a thesaurus and a dictionary.

He rolled a piece of paper into the typewriter and began to type: "Now is the time for all good men to come to the aid of the party"—over and over again as the phone continued its muffled, incessant ringing.

Then he shrugged, opened the drawer, and

grabbed the receiver. "Many times no, damn it! I promised Bea I wouldn't get involved. I don't want to get involved. Call your brother-in-law on the state police, call in the F.B.I. for violation of civil rights. Good-bye."

Before the receiver hit the cradle he heard Rocco say that he was calling from the squad car and would be at Nutmeg Hill in five minutes.

Lyon sighed and poured himself a glass of sherry.

Rocco Herbert eased his large frame into the leather chair in the corner of the study and drank his vodka neat. The single light from the desk lamp gave a diffused illumination to the room, and it made Lyon recall nights in Korea. Then, Rocco Herbert had been a Ranger captain. After intelligence-gathering missions he would come to Lyon's tent at division headquarters, and with a Coleman lantern swinging from the center pole, the two men would talk softly and drink whatever was available. As an intelligence officer, Lyon had existed on the information the large Ranger officer provided, and the relationship had grown and ripened when they discovered their mutual origins in Connecticut.

There was an immediate juxtaposition of fragmentary pictures from earlier in the day. Rocco, at the political rally on the green taking two small tow-headed children across the street, their fingers entwined in his. Rocco, kneeling, the Magnum sputtering calculated shots at spaced intervals toward the church steeple.

"I thought you'd be interested in what I've turned up so far."

"Come on, Rocco. Don't bait me like that. Bea and I knew Llewyn well. He was a friend more than a political ally of Bea's. We're as interested in your catching his killer as anyone in the state, but don't try to grapple me into this. It's headline stuff. You can get all the help you need."

"We did pretty well together the last time."

"I had a personal reason to work on the little girl's killing."

Rocco didn't answer. He poured himself another drink, sat back in the chair and twirled his glass. "Perhaps as an old friend you'd be interested in my shop talk."

"You're as obvious as a rattlesnake. What about Captain Norbert?"

"I'm only using the state police for lab work."

"Oh, great. An ego trip." Seeing Rocco wince, Lyon regretted the remark. As Murphysville's chief of police, Rocco commanded a force that sometimes totaled twelve men and was often sensitive about the mundane nature of his work.

"No, Lyon. Not an ego trip."

"I'm sorry, and I am interested in your work, but in this instance there are other considerations. Bea is understandably very upset. It was pretty damn traumatic for her to be so close to the killing. I just can't have myself involved in something so painful for her. . . . Hell, it's not my job or my duty as a citizen."

"Didn't say it was."

"You're a big boy now." That he was, Lyon thought. At six feet eight and 270 pounds, Rocco Herbert was the largest police officer in the state. "You're also a bright man who will do all anyone can."

"We found the weapon in the church. A thirty-thirty, two shots fired."

"Shell casings?"

"Two."

"I want to compliment you on your fast reaction at the green. Immediately picking out where the shots came from and returning fire must have disconcerted the sniper."

Rocco nodded noncommittally. "The lab checked out the rifle and established it as the murder weapon to the exclusion of all other rifles."

"Any prints?"

"No."

"Damn it all, Rocco. You're trying to involve me. Seriously, I have a wife who is upset, and a book to finish for a contract deadline."

"Because of his helmet, my description of the bike rider is no damn good. Of course we've made plaster casts of the tire marks. By the way, he got into the church through . . ."

Lyon swiveled his chair and began to type: "Now is the time for all good men to come to the aid of . . ."

Rocco continued, raising his voice over the typing. "Back door of the church was unlocked and the sexton was out on the green listening to the speeches."

Exasperated, Lyon turned to face Rocco. "I will talk about old army times, you can give me the latest gossip from around town, we will commiserate together over the state of the world, but no murder details."

"The selectmen are going to be mad as hell over your wrecking the squad car."

"Me wreck it! We were chasing the bastard."

"You were driving. An unauthorized driver at that. You never could drive well, Lyon."

"It wouldn't fit between the rocks."

"Shouldn't have tried," Rocco said and smiled.

"Isn't it time for you to go home?"

"I need another belt," Rocco said as he poured another drink.

"You're really hitting the stuff tonight."

The two men were quiet until Rocco eased himself from the leather chair and crossed to the fireplace. He put his glass on the mantel and ran his hand along the rough fieldstone for a moment before beginning to pace the room. "There's something . . ." His voice trailed off.

"I absolutely refuse to ask what," Lyon said and found himself discomfited by the obvious agitation in his friend. "It's not all incumbent on you, Rocco. As I said, the state has a host of back-up facilities to help you. No one in the world expects you to tackle the case with your small force."

"I have to tell you." The brittle words died away in the quiet room.

"Something I really should know?"

"I'm afraid so," Rocco said softly.

"You had better get it over with."

"It's in the car. I'll be right back."

Rocco left, and in a few minutes Lyon heard the slam of a car trunk. Fear slipped into the room. His study had always been a refuge, a place away from the world, a sanctuary which had now become filled with apprehension. He knew his friend well enough to discern that he was concerned, and that the concern dealt with Lyon.

Rocco returned carrying a large case and a portable movie screen. Wordlessly he set up the screen and positioned the projector.

"If it's pornographic I don't want to see it," Lyon said with an attempted laugh. "Unless she's terrific."

"Uh-huh," Rocco replied as he bent to plug in the movie projector.

"If it's a film monument to that great day you tagged fourteen cars for speeding on Route Sixty-six, I'm already bored."

Rocco reached over and snapped off the desk lamp and turned on the projector. "Debbie Williams took the film this afternoon at the green."

"She's only sixteen."

"I know, and the camera is one of those Kodak deals that sell for thirty or forty dollars. The state lab rushed a print for me."

They fell silent as Rocco adjusted the focus. As the film started, Lyon noticed that the camera wavered and frames blurred and sometimes slipped out of focus. He conjectured that the camera was a recent acquisition of the young girl's and that perhaps the filming of the activities on the green was her cinematic baptism.

"She got it yesterday on her birthday," Rocco said. "The camera, I mean."

"Figures," Lyon replied.

The camera panned to a beautiful, belligerent black face. "Hey, that's Kimberly Ward," Lyon said with delight. Kim lived in the apartment over the Wentworth garage with her teenage daughter. She was Bea's administrative assistant, secretary and factotum for the Wentworths—when she wasn't organizing protest marches. The camera moved from Kim's face to the placard she was carrying. It paused there for a moment, and they could read the sign:

"WELFARE LAWS ARE UNFAIR"

"I get it," Lyon said. "You're arresting Kim for unlawful protest without a permit."

"No. Just watch."

Spasmodic camera shots showed the green filling with people, the speakers arriving, and part of the speech given by the congressman. At one point the camera tilted in a skewed angle, swerved away from the speaker's platform and slid along the green, showing Amsten House and the Congregational Church. Rocco stopped the projector. He reversed the machine for a moment and then started it forward. The shots of the house and church slid past. Rocco again stopped the machine and isolated the church.

"We were able to blow this frame up," he said. "The astronomy department at the university isolated it and used a computer method developed for some of those space fly-bys. Look at the definition on the blowup." He switched on the light and propped up a fifteen-by-fourteen picture of the church.

"I can see him in there!" Lyon said. In the dark recess behind the belfry window, partway up the steeple, the definite image of a man holding a rifle could be discerned. "Too many shadows. You'll never get an ID on that."

"I know, but I thought you might like to see it."

"Hey, no kidding, Rocco. I'm not being coy. I really don't want to get involved."

"That's not why I brought this stuff here. Keep watching." He turned off the light and again started the projector. Bea was at the speaker's podium making her introductory remarks for Randolph Llewyn. Even though Lyon knew what was coming, the muscles in his stomach tightened and he could feel the perspiration forming in the palms of his hands.

As the introduction drew to a close, he could follow the movement of Bea's lips. "The camera's close in."

"First row," Rocco mumbled.

Lyon knew what Bea was saying: "A fine lawyer, dedicated family man, I give you the next governor of this state, Randolph Llewyn."

He saw his wife turn quickly and reach for Llewyn. Llewyn stood and was immediately flung backward by the impact of the bullet.

The camera pointed to the sky, and then went dark. After the shots Debbie had probably flung herself to the ground as many others had.

"I'm going to run the last few feet again," Rocco said. "In slow motion."

Again Lyon watched the film and saw Bea finish her remarks, turn quickly from the podium and reach toward Llewyn. Llewyn died again and the film was finished.

"Oh, my God," Lyon said, and knew why Rocco had wanted him to see the film.

"Yes," Rocco replied.

"Run it in slow motion again."

For the third time they watched Randolph Llewyn's last filmed moments. Lyon felt his fingers cramp as he clutched the chair arms.

Catapulting from the desk chair, he flung open the study door and staggered to the downstairs lavatory, where he vomited repeatedly into the toilet bowl. When the peristaltic motions subsided, he washed his face in very cold water, toweled himself and walked slowly back to the study.

Rocco had poured another drink.

"Do you think it's conclusive?" Lyon asked.

"I'm afraid so. I've had blowups made of the last few frames."

"I'd like to see them," Lyon said as he moved his manuscript and typewriter from the desk.

Rocco adjusted the lamp and spread the film blowups across the desk. He arranged them in frame sequence, starting at the top right-hand corner of the desk. They showed Bea's last remark, her turn, Llewyn's standing and then falling under the shot, and the second shot's point of impact.

"What's the elapsed time from this frame to this frame?" Lyon asked, pointing.

"Half a second."

"Exact distance from the steeple window to the platform?"

"Two hundred and nineteen yards."

"Scope on the rifle?"

"Yes, with windage adjusted. He knew what he was doing."

"Trigger squeeze would take—?"

"Part of a second."

Both men looked again at the movie blowups. The first shot hit Llewyn, and as he fell, Bea bent toward him. The second shot, as the pictures clearly indicated, entered a sign immediately to the rear of where Bea had been standing.

"It would have hit her neck or lower face," Lyon said in a low voice.

"I know," Rocco said and put a hand on Lyon's shoulder. "He was using a soft-nosed bullet, hollow point; it flattens on impact. One for each of them."

"He could have been a nut who didn't care."

"Do you believe that?"

"No, too much care and preparation." Lyon reached into the bottom desk drawer and took out a rolled geodetic map and a pair of dividers. "All right, let's see where the bastard was going." He unrolled the map and weighted the edges with books. He bent over the map and began to draw intersecting lines leading away from the Congregational Church and cemetery.

Both men turned with a start as the study door

banged open. Bea stood in the hallway, the bright light behind her outlining her figure through the nearly transparent nightgown.

"OH, MY GOD!" she said. "HE'S DRAWING CIRCLES ON MAPS AGAIN!"

2

"ALL RIGHT, YOU GUYS, WRAP IT UP!" Bea yelled.

"I was going to suggest the same to you, dear," Lyon said as he pointedly looked at her clearly outlined figure while Rocco diplomatically averted his eyes.

"Oh." Bea scuttled from the room. They heard her rummaging through the downstairs hall closet.

"I don't want her to know," Lyon whispered.

"Then get Bea the hell away from here for a while. Send her on a cruise, to Europe."

"She'd never go. The legislature's in special session, and the nominating convention's in a few days."

Bea came back wearing Lyon's rumpled London Fog raincoat over her nightgown. She plunked down defiantly in a chair and glared at them. "Come on, you guys. No circles on maps, no lists of suspects. YOU PROMISED ME, LYON."

"Do you want me to get your hearing aid, dear?"

"I'm not staying long enough for it; and besides, you can hear me and I don't need to hear you."

"It's settled, Beatrice," Lyon said in a low voice. "I will give Rocco any help I can in this matter."

"WHAT?"

"We're working on it together. It's settled."

"You're stubborn as hell, Wentworth. Don't you remember the last time you two worked on a case together? You were almost killed and ended up in a hospital. I can sum this all up in one word. ONE WORD."

"That's all right, dear. I can imagine."

"And as far as you're concerned, Chief Herbert, I'm calling your wife and telling her that the two of you are screwing nubile girls in Lyon's study."

She flounced from the room and slammed the door. With a worried look Rocco sank back in the chair. "Do you really think she'll call my wife?"

Lyon shook his head. "No, but she will fume for a day or two."

"You know, you're going to have to tell her some story. I've got men guarding the house."

"I'll think of something."

"Okay." The chief seemed to dismiss that portion of their discussion and leaned forward. "Here's all we have. One rifle firmly established as the murder weapon, and of course we're running a check on it, but I wouldn't count on anything from that source."

"And the tire marks, you say, are ordinary?"

"Yes. Unless we have the original motorcycle to compare them with, there's no way to trace it."

"Any evidence in the church?"

"Nothing. No prints, and no one saw him."

"You're sure it's a him?"

"Hell, we can't even establish that. You and I were the only ones who saw the killer, and I can't even establish sex. You know what my question is?"

"Why Beatrice? I don't know. I really don't. Certainly nothing in our personal life. Of course she has a great many political enemies, and there are large segments of the opposition that would be pleased as hell to have her shut up, but killing her . . . I can't believe that."

"I don't buy any maniacal nut theory."

"Me either. Rifle with scope, right angle of fire, planned escape route—hardly anything haphazard about it."

"It's got to be politically motivated. There's no other answer," Rocco said.

Scenes of angry people flashed before Lyon's eyes. Committee meetings, political meetings, forums—filled over the years with anger directed toward his wife. She took strong positions and had either staunch supporters or spiteful enemies. No individual stood out with clarity, no pictures of a potential killer. "I just don't know," he finally said.

"You could help by drawing up a list."

"I'll try. If we'd been getting threatening letters or phone calls . . . nothing like that has happened."

Rocco stood. "Why don't you think on it? Maybe one of us will come up with something." Lyon, staring out the window into the darkness, didn't answer. "Take this." Rocco pulled a .32 automatic from his jacket pocket and handed it butt first to Lyon. "Come down to my office in the morning and we'll fix you up with a permit."

Lyon took the gun gingerly. "I don't want it."

"I'd rather you did. You know how to use it."

"Of course, but still—"

"Keep it. See you in the morning."

The police chief lumbered from the room, and Lyon heard him quietly close the outside door. He sat looking at the weapon in his hand.

The phone's ring cut through his groggy sleep. He stretched uncomfortably in the leather chair and massaged a crick in his neck. He wondered what the phone company would do if he blew up the local transmission lines. He reached for the receiver.

"Thornburton here. Do you know what else Robin wants to do?"

"I haven't seen her in a couple of years, Stacey. The last time she was here, I think she wanted to be an astronaut."

"Be a sculptor! She wants to build big damn statues like the Russkies do. You know the kind, men beating plowshares into rifles, that sort of thing."

"I'm not quite sure it goes that way."

"Next, she'll turn pinko."

"You're a fine artist, Stacey. One of the best illustrators in the business. She's trying to follow in your—"

"Don't say it, Wentworth. Get yourself another boy. I'm sending the outline back. My next project is going to be a portfolio of posthumous Medal of Honor winners in action."

"Stacey, you never got within twenty miles of the front."

"That's below the belt, Wentworth. Really, below the belt."

The phone clicked dead. He turned to see Bea

examining the photographs spread across the desk. "Bea."

"If you'd finish the book and send him a final copy to work on, we'd all be better off," she said without turning from her inspection of the pictures Rocco had left.

"Bea."

"I was lonely upstairs alone," she said in a soft voice, without turning. "I came down to get you."

"I must have fallen asleep."

She turned to face him. Her eyes were wide, her face chalky as she went to him and took the .32 from his fingers. "Falling asleep with a gun is dangerous. You could shoot your toe off or some other dumb thing."

Lyon took the gun back and slammed it into the center desk drawer. "Let's go back to bed."

"Yes," she replied distantly. "I looked at the pictures. Taken from a movie film, huh?"

"Oh, those, yes. Debbie what's-her-name had a camera, and you know how Rocco is, he wanted me to see them."

"It was meant for me too, wasn't it?"

"No. He just thought I might see something in them that—"

"The bullet. The bullet that missed me. I can look at these things and see that."

"A haphazard thing," he mumbled.

"Llewyn was killed and I was supposed to be too."

"Bea, please."

"Oh, my God, Lyon. I'm scared."

"There are two policemen outside the house right now."

"What about tomorrow, the day after?"

"We'll find him, her, whoever it is. I promise you, Bea. We'll find him."

"I demand my rights."

Lyon Wentworth sat bolt upright in bed and tried to reach for a weapon before his eyes focused and he saw Kimberly Ward's angry black face bent over the bed.

"Damn it all, Kim. We have rights too. We're in bed."

Bea untwined herself from Lyon and sat up groggily.

"I demand a lawyer," Kim said. "I will not tolerate any more of this surveillance."

"What in hell are you talking about?"

"Damn it, Kim, do you have to protest in our bedroom at"—Bea looked at the small electric clock on the night table—"at seven in the morning?"

"Damn right!" Kim yelled. "The fuzz is staked out in the yard. Two pigs. One in the back and one in the front. They even changed shifts a few minutes ago."

"That's not surveillance on you, Kim," Lyon said.

"That big buddy of yours is behind this. Old Super Pig is after my butt."

"It's not what you think."

"They said they'd get me after my equalization of unemployment benefits protest."

"Why don't we have breakfast and talk about it?" Lyon suggested as he heaved himself out of bed, then retreated rapidly when he realized he was stark naked.

"Oh," Kim said quietly into her coffee after Lyon and Bea outlined the situation for her. "I guess we had all better do something."

"It might be a good idea if you took a long visit with your aunt in Hartford," Bea suggested.

"No way," Kim retorted. Her eyes glinted angrily. "I think we had better get shotguns. That's what they used on the Attica brothers."

"How about a machine gun on the parapet?" Lyon suggested.

"That's silly," Bea retorted. "I was thinking of V-2s in the vestibule."

"You're both nuts," Kim said.

"WE'RE OPEN TO SUGGESTIONS, KIMBERLY," Bea shouted, and then adjusted her hearing aid.

"Take to ground," Kim said, "I know a couple of safe houses that we've used where no one will ever find you."

"I'm afraid to ask whom you've hidden," Lyon mumbled.

"I am not going to sneak away," Bea said. "I will not cower under the table or take off to Europe. Life will go on as it always has."

"You're not going to the special session of the legislature?" Kim asked.

"Of course."

"Rocco suggested last night that we might make up a list of possible political enemies for him to work on."

"Past, present or future?" Bea asked. "That would take a city directory, but it would be bipartisan."

"That's what I was afraid of," Lyon said.

Bea finished her coffee and stood up. "All right, everyone, we have lots to do today."

"Sandbag the windows?" Kim asked.

"No, my dear," Bea replied. "You and I have a lot of work to do on a gun-legislation bill that I'm going to attach as a rider to their silly sales-tax increase. Lyon has to lock himself in the study and make us all a living."

"I thought I'd take a flight this morning," Lyon said.

"Oh, no." Bea sank back in her chair. "Not that."

"Want to come? It's very relaxing and a wonderful time to sort things out."

"The last flight you took ended up in the Connecticut River."

"That wasn't all my fault. Will you two help me get off the ground?"

"Do we have a choice?"

"No."

They trundled the hot-air balloon from the barn at the rear of the house and spread the balloon evenly along the ground. As Bea held the bottom aperture open, Lyon braced the propane burner against his hip and shot jagged spurts of flame into the bag. As the air began to heat, the large bag filled and slowly rose. They scurried around the perimeter, unfolding the creases so that it filled quickly and evenly.

As the balloon envelope took shape and began to lift lazily from the ground, the huge dimensions of Lyon's major book characters began to form. Painted by Stacey Thornburton during his last visit to Connecticut at the cost of three bottles of Jack Daniel's, the two immense Wobblies curved around the balloon to join hands (or paws) over the legend, WOBBLY II.

With the bag firmly held to the ground by mooring lines, the small wicker basket danced a few feet off the surface. Lyon walked slowly around the filling balloon and checked the bag for wear and leaks and occasionally tugged on ropes to make sure that all was secure. As he climbed into the gondola, he adjusted the flow of propane on the burner immediately below the bag's appendix. He made other preflight checks and waved to the waiting women who held the mooring lines.

The lines were released, and as he reeled them into the basket, the balloon began its slow ascent.

At 650 feet he again adjusted the propane burner, released a smidgin of hot air from the bag, and leveled his altitude. In the yard below, the women waved and slowly began to walk back to the house. It seemed obvious from their body language that they were animatedly arguing—and then it occurred to him that gun legislation wouldn't be Kim's cup of tea, to say the least.

The bag drifted slowly in the almost windless day, and Lyon leaned over the edge of the basket to watch the moving panorama below. Their house, Nutmeg Hill, sat solidly on its granite base on the promontory overlooking the river, its four chimneys pointing stalwartly toward the sky and bracketing the widow's walk. Not that the house was that large; in fact it had been a rather rambling, falling-down house when they purchased and began to renovate it.

On the river below, as it wound its way toward Long Island Sound, a few pleasure boats made white wakes. Over to the left was the Congregational Church and the town green. He made out workmen removing yesterday's speaker's platform. In back of the church was the cemetery and the rising meadow that had been the scene of the futile chase.

Over the hill beyond the meadow were several roads, any one of which could have been the route of the killer's retreat. Which one?

Temporarily, he had to put aside the all-consuming fear for his wife's safety and attempt to come up with something that would aid Rocco Herbert; for in the ultimate scheme of things only the capture of the killer would guarantee Bea's safety.

A mild westerly wind had begun to move the balloon back on its original path. His quick calculation indicated that in minutes he'd be back over the house. Suddenly, he wanted to descend. He wanted to descend as quickly as he could.

Diocletian's Cycle and Drag Shop on Route 66 was squeezed between an auto junk yard and a stone mason's shop. Lyon turned the pickup into the narrow dirt drive and parked in front of the rusting Quonset hut.

Four members of a cycle club, wearing their colors, were revving Harley 1200s in front of the building. Emblazoned with sequins on the back of their leather jackets were the words, "Krauts M.C., Breeland, Ct."

Lyon left the truck, ignored the somewhat hostile glances cast his way by the Krauts, and entered the building. Inside, motorcycles of all shapes and sizes cluttered the floor, while to the rear of the building two men were working on disassembled machines in a repair area. A bearded man in white coveralls with the name Diocletian labeled in blue over his pocket left a workbench and slouched toward Lyon.

"Mr. Diocletian?"

"Everyone calls me D."

"I wonder if I might rent a trail bike for the day."

"You've got to be kidding."

"Not really."

"Listen, buddy. The last guy I rented a bike to was wanted on six counts of carnal knowledge. Three months later they found the bike in Portland."

"Portland's only the next town over."

"Portland, Oregon."

"Anybody you know rent them?"

"You might try Crazy Louis down in Danbury. He'll do most anything for a buck."

"But you're not sure?"

"Not unless somebody's gone wacko recently."

"What's the cheapest motorcycle you could sell me?"

"For trails?"

"That's what I had in mind."

Diocletian's face seemed to merge through several contortions as he fought valiantly to keep greed from becoming too obvious. "I do have one nice model over in the corner."

Lyon followed him toward the rear of the shop where a peeling red and greasy motorcycle was propped among some cobwebs in the corner. "Does it run?" he asked.

"Like a baby. Four fifty and it's yours."

"Three hundred and you've got a deal."

"Sold."

"How about showing me how to start the thing?"

"You got a cycle license?"

"I've had a driver's license for years."

"No, in this state you've got to take a separate test and driver's examination for a cycle license."

"I didn't know that. But what if I just run over back trails?"

"In that case the cops will never catch you."

"So I've recently noticed," Lyon replied.

In front of the Quonset hut, under the bemused glares of the Krauts M.C., Diocletian gave Lyon a quick lesson in the operation of the trail bike. For another five dollars he threw in a board that could be utilized to push the cycle on and off the back of the pickup. When Lyon felt he had a vague idea of its operation, he loaded the cycle on the pickup and drove from the store.

As he pulled onto the highway, he felt proud of his bargaining powers in lowering the price of the motorcycle. For a brief moment he thought he heard gales of laughter coming from the Quonset hut, but he chose to ignore it.

He off-loaded the motorcycle from the truck at the rear of the Congregational Church by the green. Before mounting the machine, he paused, had a thought, and walked around the corner of the church back to the green and entered the Murphysville Hardware and Supply Company.

Dan Lufkin shook his head and smiled as Lyon entered the store. "If you're after fuses again, Lyon . . . if I told you once I've told you four times that you've got circuit breakers up at Nutmeg Hill."

"Very funny, Dan. How about selling me some ammunition?"

"If you want ammo for your books, you need a wooden stake or silver bullets."

"If you read my books, Dan, you'd know I don't write monster stories."

"What I heard."

"How about some ammo?"

"Sure, what kind you want?"

"Thirty-thirty."

"Don't have it."

"You didn't even look."

"Don't need to."

"How come?"

"Well, in the first place, people who have that kind of gun use it to go to Maine or Canada for deer or bear. No call for me to sell it. You want shotgun shells, all kinds, or .22 all kinds, you're in the right place."

"Do you require identification from anyone buying ammunition?"

"Driver's license, and they just sign the ammo register."

"That's all?"

"Couldn't be simpler, but like I say, don't get no call for thirty-thirty shells. Now, if you want a wooden stake . . ." Dan Lufkin began to laugh as Lyon left the store.

He kicked the motorcycle, which he had aptly termed the Red Devil, into life. Dirty exhaust came from the tail pipe; the machine coughed, sputtered, and finally labored into erratic life. Lyon revved the engine as he'd seen the Krauts do, released the brakes and threw it into gear.

With the front wheels off the ground, the machine sprang ahead. As he skidded across the church parking lot in a direct trajectory toward the cemetery fence, he eased off on the accelerator handle and slowed the machine until the wheels came down. He barely managed to skid through the fence opening into the cemetery.

The motorcycle wobbled as he fought for control. At one point, as the cycle barely made a sharp swerve, his leg brushed against the marker of Jeremiah Benton, 1714-1786. With relief he saw the gate at the end of the cemetery directly in front of him. He went through in a flurry of dust and started up the meadow toward a cow.

As the incline of the meadow increased, he found it necessary to speed up in order to keep his forward momentum. He sped over hillocks and small rocks, all the while attempting to avoid large boulders that were strewn haphazardly in the knee-high grass.

Without difficulty the cycle went through the dual rock formation that had stopped the police car the day before. Beyond that obstacle the ground seemed to disappear as the bike took off from a small hummock. He hit with a bone-jarring bounce; the motorcycle skidded sideways as he struggled to regain his balance. It stalled out, and he gratefully put both feet on firm ground. His hands were trembling from clenching the handlebars. He wished he had walked the trail rather than attempting to negotiate it on the bike.

On the leading edge of the hill the cowpath forked to the right and left. Which way would he have gone? The left fork was closer, but after the jump at the top of the hill it seemed unlikely that he could have negotiated the sharp turn to the left so quickly—it had to be to the right. He kicked the motorcycle alive and started slowly toward the right fork.

After a quarter of a mile the path widened and turned steeply toward a road several hundred yards farther on. He slowed and stopped at the edge of the pavement. It was a narrow, winding country road. Yesterday's rider could have turned either way. From the map examination he and Rocco had made, and also from the balloon observation, he knew that to the right the road wound through the country past a few working farms and ended at the Shady Heights subdivision. To the left, it continued through the hills for three miles until it connected with Route 90, which ran along the river. Route 90 interconnected with the Interstate and would be an obvious escape route.

He kicked the motorcycle starter and moved

slowly to the left. After the murder and the abortive chase, Rocco had radioed instructions to his small force and to the state police. They would have established road blocks, or at least check points, near the Interstate connection. Any cyclist would have been stopped. Unless the killer had done exactly what he had done—used a truck to transport the trail bike.

He slowed the motorcycle to a near stall and began to examine the dirt shoulder at the edge of the road. Within fifty yards he found what he was looking for. A vehicle had been pulled off onto the shoulder. He stopped the bike and got off to kneel by the side of the road next to a small oil spot. The single track of the bike was clearly visible as it approached the dual tracks of the other vehicle. He recalled that the day before yesterday it had rained: the tracks must have been made in the last forty-eight hours. The cycle tracks ended a few feet before the other vehicle tracks. The killer had obviously loaded the trail bike onto a small truck or van parked on the shoulder.

The supposition would be verified when Rocco's men made molds of the tire marks and compared them to the ones found in back of the church. It also gave them one more fact to work with—an additional fact that might allow them to make another conjecture toward another fact.

He was in a hurry to get back to town. He started the motorcycle and decided to avoid the difficult trail through the meadow by going down the road to Route 90 and back that way to Rocco's office. The escape route was verified, and there was also an additional lead among the things he had heard today.

With its operator lost in thought, the motorcycle failed to negotiate the sharp right turn, crashed through a thin wooden retaining fence and shot off into space. Lyon found himself separating from the mottled red cycle as they both dropped into the waters of an abandoned quarry.

"Those wet clothes are going to mark the bench," Rocco Herbert said as Lyon scowled.

It had been a two-mile walk to Sarge's Bar and Grill, off Route 90. He had ordered a double sherry and called Rocco from the pay phone. Now, as the chief sat across from him in the scarred wooden booth and nursed a beer, Lyon heard himself squish loudly as he shifted position.

"That quarry's dangerous," he said. "Kids could get killed out there."

"To my recollection you're the only one who ever ran a motorcycle into it. Who in hell do you think you are—Evel Knievel?"

"I was thinking."

"Oh, Jesus, typical. You know, of course, that we'll never get your plaything out of there."

"Well, it wasn't much of a machine anyway."

"I've sent two men out to make a cast of those tracks you found, although I don't see how it's going to help us."

"One more thing to work with."

"All right, you took a ride over the meadow, probably duplicated the killer's route. You found cycle tracks stopping next to the tracks of another vehicle . . . fine, he probably loaded the trail bike onto a covered van. That would get him past any check points we managed to set up. I still don't see where that puts us."

"What about the rifle?" Lyon asked.

"Stolen three days ago from a home in Hartford."

"Was ammunition taken at the same time?"

"Ammo? I don't know." Rocco pulled a Xerox copy of a report from his pocket and quickly scanned it. "This is a copy of the investigating officer's report concerning the theft. Nothing at all was taken except the rifle and scope."

"It's unlikely that the burglar knew exactly what kind of rifle he was going to get."

"True."

"Which means that he wouldn't necessarily have the proper caliber ammunition available, nor the time to make a trip out of state to purchase some."

"So, you can buy ammo at most hardware stores, discount houses, sporting-goods stores . . . there's probably tens of dozens of places in a fifty-mile radius."

"Exactly," Lyon said. "And only dozens."

"What are you driving at?"

"Let's create a matrix of probabilities. Now, when you buy ammunition you sign a register."

"And can easily use a false name."

"Why bother? The dealer asks to see a driver's license as identification. Why bother with false ID when you're buying something that's seemingly as innocuous as ammuniton that's available to anyone?"

"So our killer buys thirty-thirty ammo, signs the book with his own name. How in hell can we track that down when we don't know who he is?"

"Hear me out. In this state, hunting is illegal with anything but a shotgun."

"Right."

"In addition, buying shells in July for a trip to Maine to hunt bear or deer which are out of season is unlikely. That means our killer is one of a few who are buying that type of cartridge at this time of year."

"Someone could buy a rifle in preparation for the

hunting season and buy cartridges at the same time, or a nonhunter, a marksman, might want ammunition at any time of year."

"That's only part of it. Operating a motorcycle requires a special kind of license from the motor vehicle department."

"Yes. I *am* a police officer, Lyon."

"Now, suppose we get a list of persons who've bought thirty-caliber ammunition in the northern part of the state during the past several days and run those names through the motor-vehicle department computer to match with licensed motorcyclists."

Rocco drummed his fingers on the tabletop and stared off into space for a moment. "He could be from out of state, not a licensed cyclist; a lot of variables."

"It's all we have," Lyon said.

"Damn it, you've got a point. There can't be that many places selling thirty-thirty ammo at this time of year, and matching those names against the registered cyclists won't be difficult. It just might work."

Lyon sat back and sipped on his sherry. "Then you'll try it?"

"Damn right, I will." Rocco Herbert pulled a summons pad from his breast pocket. "Just one thing."

"What's that?"

"Do you have a cycle license?"

"Of course not."

Rocco wrote out a ticket and handed it across the table. "Circuit Court Fourteen in two weeks. Driving without a proper operator's permit."

3

"YOU WHAT WITH THREE HUNDRED DOLLARS AND THEN DROPPED IT IN THE QUARRY?"

Lyon Wentworth drove with one hand, reached across the seat toward his wife and turned up her hearing aid. "For a good cause, darling." He turned his eyes back toward the road and steered the red Datsun through the light summer rain.

Bea gave a slight groan and leaned back against the headrest. "I wanted to re-cover the living-room couch," she said in a small voice.

"To make it short, Rocco is running a check against everyone who's bought thirty-thirty cartridges since the theft of the rifle and comparing that list against the registered motorcyclists in the state."

"Don't forget to take out a state lottery ticket; your odds are better."

"Not really. If you break it down, how many people in a small state like Connecticut can fall into both categories?"

"I hope you're right. I'm getting tired of having our friends in blue always around."

As Lyon glanced in the rear-view mirror he could see the prowl car following them at a not-so-discreet thirty yards. "If we'd stayed home tonight instead of going to this party, we wouldn't have an escort."

"They'd be out in the bushes."

"Maybe we should be thankful. Hey, do we really have to go to this thing? Damn, I hate cocktail parties."

"You mean you hate political cocktail parties."

"With us, it's always the same thing."

"How about those literary things you drag me to in New York?"

"That's only once a year. Who's going to be there tonight?"

"Our fearless majority leader, Big Mouth Mackay."

"Rustling support for his candidacy?"

"They don't even wait for the body to get cold. Everyone knew I was backing Llewyn, and I've already had calls asking me to switch support to Mackay."

"Well," Lyon said as he turned into the long driveway, "I do get a kick out of Dawkins's Castle; the evening won't be a complete loss."

Dawkins's Castle wasn't a castle, although it pretended to be. Built fifty years earlier by Colonel Dawkins out of massive blocks of rock from a nearby quarry, it perched on a high promontory over the river and was a skewed cross between a Rhine castle and something angry children might build on a sandy beach.

The colonel had been dead ten years, and now the house was occupied by his son Wilkie, who, although not adding to the massive stone exterior, had filled the interior with an abundance of electronic gadgetry.

Lyon stopped before the lighted portico, and together he and Bea ran through the summer rain toward the protection of the house. Lyon raised the heavy knocker and let it fall while Bea peered at the several cars parked in the wide drive. "Mackay's already here."

"Advance and be recognized," a voice said from a speaker above the door.

"The Wentworths," Lyon replied, and almost instantly the large double doors swung open. The couple stepped into a long hallway where recessed lights in the stone walls cast a dim illumination across the tiled floor.

A wheelchair swung into sight at the end of the hall. The man in the chair pressed a small button on the arm, and the massive doors swung silently shut behind them.

"If Igor takes my raincoat, I'm leaving," Lyon said.

"Be quiet and act political or something," Bea whispered.

Wilkie Dawkins waved to them. "Welcome to the sanctuary, you two." Like many other paraplegics, he had a massive torso and muscle-knotted shoulders, and his useless legs dangled on the supporting rim of the chair. In his late thirties, he had a calculating look, with piercing eyes that were often disconcerting, and a shock of dark hair that jutted over his forehead. He extended a massive hand toward Lyon.

"Lyon, you rat fink, when are you going to write some decent pornography instead of that juvenile crap?"

"Next week," Lyon replied as he tried to slide his fingers from the crushing grip.

"How are you, Wilkie?" Bea asked as she bent over to be bussed.

"Fine, fine." Wilkie's chair whirred quietly across the carpet, through another set of doors that opened automatically, and into the living room.

A small group of somber people stood by the huge fireplace holding drinks and talking in low tones. Lyon recognized Ted Mackay, senate majority leader; Congressman Dolan, a state committeeman, and the minority leader of the House. The group peeled open as Bea approached, and as plankton are gulped by large fishes, she was absorbed immediately into the conversation.

Lyon crossed to the built-in bar at the corner of the room, where Danny Nemo was efficiently shaking cocktails. He smiled as Lyon slipped onto a stool.

"Dry Sack, Mr. Wentworth?" he asked with a smile. Danny always seemed to be smiling. Like the former tennis player and surfer that he was, he affably and ingenuously radiated health and exuberance. He had been a noncom in Wilkie Dawkins's Vietnam infantry company, and after Dawkins had received massive shrapnel wounds from an enemy rocket, Danny had carried him through enemy fire to the evac helicopter. Since then, he had remained in Dawkins's employ as butler, social secretary, barkeeper and friend. He placed Lyon's sherry on the bar and picked up his shaker.

"How's everything, Danny?" Lyon asked.

"Couldn't be better in some ways, but everyone's still upset over Randy Llewyn getting it."

Lyon nodded as Danny placed several cocktail glasses on a silver tray, expertly poured until liquor brimmed the rim of each glass and, with Lyon following, carried the tray toward the main group.

Congressman Dolan snatched a glass from the tray and sloshed liquor over his fingertips. "It's a damn conspiracy," he said. "Those radicals ought to be tracked down like dogs and annihilated."

"No one has ever proved a conspiracy since Booth's attempted coup against Lincoln," Bea said evenly.

"I think we should consider preventive detention for the far-out groups," Ted Mackay said.

"Come on, Senator. Even you don't really believe that," Bea said.

"I'm reflecting some of the thinking of this group, Beatrice."

Wilkie Dawkins held up both hands. "Ladies and gentlemen, I don't know if there's a conspiracy involved here or not, and for the time being I believe we should leave the whole matter in the hands of the proper authorities, where it belongs. We're here tonight to fill the void left by Randy Llewyn. The convention's in a few days, and unless we're careful we'll have floor fights that will divide the party—and we all know what happened last time we were divided. The opposition walked over us in November."

There were nods of assent. "I'm with Ted Mackay," Dolan said.

"Ted appreciates that," Wilkie replied. "Now, with Randy gone, we all know how it breaks out. Support is evenly divided between Ted and Mattaloni; the deciding factor rests with Senator Wentworth."

"This isn't fair, Wilkie," Bea said. "You invited

me here for a discussion on convention planning. You have no right to put me in this position at this time."

"I never knew you were afraid of taking a position on anything, Senator Wentworth," Ted Mackay said with a smile.

"Nor you to avoid taking one," Bea retorted.

"Like the welfare laws, Senator?"

The majority leader had subtly moved toward the fireplace and assumed a pose that was an effortless but effective way to dominate the group's conversation. His shock of dusty white hair, his gleaming teeth and his rugged features made Ted Mackay look like a candidate for a cigarette commercial, or, physically, like the perfect political candidate.

"That's a good example, Ted," Bea said. "Your position on the flat-grant welfare laws . . . *you* try to live in Darien, Connecticut, on three forty a month; you can't even rent a store front in Darien for that."

"If you're on welfare you sure as hell shouldn't live on the gold coast," Ted said.

Bea turned toward the rest of the group. "Well, our leader has at last taken a stand. An untenable one, but at least a position."

"Call it what you want, Bea, but at least it's consistent. You seemingly want to increase social programs and yet reduce taxes. Now that doesn't make any sense."

"I'm for a more equitable distribution."

"Soak the rich."

"I didn't say that."

"With your pendulum record, Senator, I don't know what you're saying," Mackay said with a half smile.

Lyon watched his wife approach the majority leader, and he mouthed her next remark silently as she spoke it aloud. "Now wait just a minute, Senator."

Lyon retreated across the room toward the bar where Danny Nemo stood smiling and holding a bottle of Dry Sack sherry in the air. He poured as Lyon listened to snatches of the argument taking place across the room by the fireplace.

"Welfare and higher taxes are inextricably tied together, Senator Wentworth."

"The day I vote property over people is the day I retire to my knitting," Bea retorted.

"Is that a promise?"

Lyon felt a hand on his arm and turned to see Wilkie Dawkins, who had moved noiselessly across the room in his wheelchair. "Can I see you in my study, Lyon?"

As Lyon followed the wheelchair across the room to the study, doors opened automatically and closed behind them after they had entered. The juxtaposition in this large house of feudal construction and electronic wizardry never ceased to amaze Lyon. He sat in a high-backed chair as Wilkie glided his wheelchair behind the broad oak desk.

They looked at each other for that brief moment of measurement and appraisal which determines the makeup of an imperceptible chemistry that would either attract or repel. Lyon found the brief span inconclusive.

He knew that after Dawkins's return from Vietnam as a cripple, there had been months of brooding within the castle, and then a total immersion in countless activities. Using the rather large fortune left from his father's insurance-company interests, Dawkins had founded the Murphysville Children's Museum and become the largest contributor to Bea's political party. And yet, Lyon felt, the rush of activities had only submerged the bitterness, not dissipated it.

He also felt that Dawkins considered him somewhat of an ineffectual person labeled "Bea Wentworth's husband"; a quiet man who shadowed his wife to political meetings, often seemed bored, attentive to his wife, but out of the mainstream.

"I thought perhaps you could give me a little help in dealing with Bea." He smiled. "What are we going to do with her?"

Lyon looked at the man behind the desk and debated about returning the smile. He did smile. "I hadn't really thought about it tonight, Wilkie. Last week I considered turning her in for an eighteen-year-old blonde, but she objected."

Wilkie pushed a tiled box across the desk and deftly flipped the lid to reveal small black cigars. Lyon shook his head.

"It's convention time," said Wilkie. "With Llewyn gone, the whole party is up in the air."

"He was a fine man and would have made a good governor," Lyon responded.

Wilkie shrugged. "I agree with you, but I'm also a pragmatist. I lost too many friends in Vietnam; perhaps my sensibilities have been dulled. I have to deal with the 'now' questions, and as a member of the state committee, it's my duty to create order and organization out of what's left."

"And this is where we come to Bea?"

"She controls enough delegate votes to make her important. Not enough to clinch the nomination for her choice, but sufficient to constitute a swing element at the convention."

"You know as well as I do that with Llewyn dead she leans toward Mattaloni."

"Just as it's no secret that my full support goes to Ted Mackay. If Beatrice switches her support, we have a potential first-ballot victory on the gubernatorial nomination without any internecine party fights. Ted neatly walks away with it, and that means there's a strong possibility that Bea could be the next secretary of the state."

"She's often a contender, never a nominee."

"It would make the ticket stronger. We'll even let Mattaloni have the lieutenant governor's slot."

"You heard them out there, Wilkie. She and Ted just don't get along. Bea takes strong positions and fights for them. Ted never makes a stand."

"He'll be harder for the opposition to attack."

"What's to attack?"

"I'm not asking them to crawl into bed. Just a switch of her support, and perhaps give the nominating speech for Ted."

"You had better talk to her yourself."

"I have. I thought I'd made a little headway, and then see what happens the very next time she and Ted get together."

"Bea and I only have one rule of marriage, Wilkie. She doesn't write my books and I don't run her political campaigns."

"Even if it meant Washington in two years?"

The Wobblies in the White House as a possible book flashed to Lyon. He snapped himself back to reality and laughed. "Even so."

The study door slammed against the wall as Ted Mackay strode into the room. "That broad's got to go!"

Lyon stood to face the irate state senator. "I find that in extremely poor taste."

"Taste! Christ! She's ripping me apart in front of my own supporters. What is this, a debate?"

"Calm down," Wilkie said. "There's an answer to everything, and it's a question of making the right deal for Bea."

"You can't make deals with her. She's nuts."

"She'd strengthen your ticket as secretary of the state."

"Crap! I want no part of her."

"I've had enough of that, Ted!" Lyon said as his anger rose.

Ted turned to him and smiled as he put his arm on Lyon's shoulder. Lyon back-stepped. "It's only politics, Lyon. You know that under different circumstances Bea is one of my favorite persons, but our chemistry is wrong politically."

"Then we'll make it right," Wilkie said.

"No."

"What?"

Mackay sat back in an easy chair and looked levelly at Wilkie. "I said no, Wilkie. I've always appreciated your support, but on this I'm adamant."

"You'll do exactly as I say, Ted—exactly."

"Don't push me, Wilkie. I'm in no mood to be pushed."

Lyon felt an interplay between the two men that to his knowledge had never before existed. He raised his glass. "I think I'll get a refill."

As the study doors closed, he had a last glimpse of Wilkie Dawkins brooding behind the desk. He took Bea's arm and steered her toward a secluded corner away from the remainder of the group, which had broken into pro-Mackay or -Wentworth factions.

"Do you realize that you're blowing your chances of being the first woman President?"

"Dawkins got to you."

"Right, he thinks I'd make a great first lady."

"If I lay off Mackay and vote for him?"

"You're terribly astute."

"Are you serious?"

"No."

"Oh, Jesus," Bea said as she looked over Lyon's shoulder. "Your large friend is here."

Lyon felt a hand on his shoulder and turned to face Rocco Herbert. "How in hell do you always know where we are?"

"I've got two men following you, or hadn't you noticed?"

"Noticed? They're about as subtle as the seventh cavalry."

"It worked," Rocco said.

"You've got a feedback from the MVD computer?"

"On the nose. We ran a match on everyone who signed for thirty-caliber ammo and ran it against the registered motorcyclists."

"And you came up with seven hundred names?" Bea asked.

"Would you believe one? Junior Haney, age twenty-eight, lives in Breeland. Three nolles for theft—auto and a B and E conviction on his record."

"Address?"

"Current as of a month ago."

"You bring him in?"

"You know I wouldn't make a move without you, Lyon," Rocco said and laughed.

"You really think it's him?" Bea asked.

"It's all we have so far," Rocco replied. "We'll see what we can turn up when we interview him."

4

It was a black-and-white morning. The leaden sky cast a dull sheen across the road as Rocco accelerated the cruiser toward eighty . He drove effortlessly with one hand, and with the other, switched on the blinking roof light.

"Are you sure you don't want the siren?" Lyon grimaced as he clutched his seat belt.

"If my driving bothers you, why do you come?"

"I'm a masochist. If you're in such a hurry, we could have done this last night."

"A name appearing on two lists hardly constitutes grounds for an arrest. An interview, a few questions—but there's no need to dawdle."

A passing state police car blinked its lights in recognition of the Murphysville cruiser as the speedometer steadied on eighty.

Breeland was a factory town twenty miles from Murphysville. They'd checked the large map in Rocco's office before leaving, and Lyon had scribbled directions to the street that the motor-vehicle department had given as the last known address of Junior Haney.

As they exited off the Interstate, they crossed a rusting iron bridge spanning a muddy river. Breeland was a depressing town, one of many Connecticut cities formed in the early 1800s that now dotted the landscape between the hills along rivers that once were the source of power for textile plants and knitting mills. Connecticut tinkers no longer walked the land to the west, while knitting and textile mills had moved south years ago. Half the factories had closed; the remaining half manufactured precision tools and gauges. Clapboard houses spotted the hills in stagnant display.

As Lyon called off directions from his notes, Rocco slowed to a rational speed. When they made the last turn toward 2339 Halliburton Court, they found that the address was contained within a low-cost housing development. The grass between the peeling frame buildings was too high to be neat and not high enough to be termed overgrown. Sullen children stared at the police car with undisguised contempt.

The doorbell of 2339 was immovable, and Rocco knocked loudly. Dishes clattered inside the apartment and a small child began to wail. Rocco knocked again.

The young woman who opened the door had been pretty last year. She wore a brief halter and faded denim pants. A wisp of hair curled over her slightly perspiring forehead, and she pushed it back in a nervous gesture. Her eyes dulled as she looked past them toward the police car parked at the curb.

"Yes?"

"I'm looking for Junior Haney. Is he home?"

"He's at work."

"I'm Chief Rocco Herbert. I'd like to talk to you. You're—?"

"Loyce Haney," she answered in a low voice as she stepped aside for them to enter. "I told you, Junior's not here."

The front door opened directly into a small living room; a kitchen area was visible to the rear, with an unkempt bedroom beyond that. The plastic-covered furniture had begun to show wear. A petulant baby dressed in a diaper sat in a playpen, half-crying as he looked at them. Dominating the far wall of the room was a large combination color television and stereo set.

As Rocco and Lyon looked toward the television set, Loyce Haney stepped in front of them as if to block their view of the baroque cabinet.

"Junior's got a receipt for the TV. He showed it to me."

"Does he have a receipt for the rifle?" Rocco asked.

"Junior don't have no gun."

"Someone told me he did."

"Someone told you wrong. Hey, you're not Breeland police. That patch on your shoulder says Murphysville. You got no rights here."

"I can call the locals if you want, Mrs. Haney."

She shrugged, sank back on the couch and lit a cigarette. Lyon wondered how long she could have been married. Two years, three at the most; she couldn't be much over twenty. Behind her tired eyes he saw the girl she might have been two years ago. A girl riding behind Junior on his motorcycle, her arms around his waist, an overt sensuality about her, filled with the dreams of the times, until she offered Junior the poor girl's dowry—his child.

"Junior's been clean for months," she said. "He's been working regular at the station."

"What station?"

"The Exxon on Cumberland Street."

"He's there now?"

"Since seven this morning."

"He took his cycle to work?"

"Only way to get there; it's five miles from here."

"The TV set new?"

"I told you. He has a receipt for it. The store even delivered it here themselves, adjusted the color and everything."

"On a charge account?"

"It's all paid for. We got the receipt."

"When?"

"The other day. It's brand new."

"A thousand dollars?"

"Twelve hundred."

"He must be working a lot of overtime."

"He came into some money."

"Where's the rifle?"

"I told you. No gun."

"Where was he the day before yesterday?"

"At work. I'm not going to answer any more questions." She crushed her cigarette out in a souvenir ash tray and crossed to the playpen, where she picked up the baby and held it tightly against her breasts. "Go away. Just go away and leave me alone. Junior didn't do nothing. He told me he didn't."

Loyce Haney rocked back and forth, clutching the baby as though her maternity were a protective mantle.

"All right, Mrs. Haney," Rocco said softly.

"Thank you for your time." He turned and strode from the apartment. Lyon stood in the center of the room for a moment, and as he looked at the tired young woman before her large television, he wished for her sake that it wasn't Junior. He turned and followed Rocco to the car.

They pulled onto the gas-station apron on Cumberland Street to find an El Dorado at the pumps. Its driver honked impatiently for service. Then with a screech of tires the El Dorado pulled away from the station.

The service-bay doors were open, a Chevy was on the grease rack, and the door to the office was unlocked. No attendants were visible.

"Anybody home?" Rocco called as he walked through the empty station.

"The phone," Lyon said as he indicated the wall pay-telephone.

"She called him."

"We should have expected that."

"It still doesn't prove he's our man, although I'd bet a thousand to one that the money for the TV didn't come from working here."

"We trace him to his home, his wife calls ahead, and he takes off with the money from his job," Lyon said as he shut the empty cash-register drawer. "Seems to me he was in a hurry."

"Too much of a hurry to take his colors. That's a real hurry."

"His what?" Lyon asked.

"His colors," Rocco said as he held up a leather jacket that hung on a nail in the corner of the small office. Krauts M.C. was emblazoned on the back of the jacket.

55

Captain Sean Murdock of the Breeland Police Department was short and squat, with a round face laced with red lines, and mean as hell. He pointed a fat forefinger at two chairs in his small office and scowled across the desk at his visitors.

"Who the hell is Captain Norbert of the state police?" he snapped.

"My brother-in-law," Rocco replied. "Why?"

"We put out the APB on Junior Haney, like you asked, and five minutes later I get a call from state police barracks, from this joker Norbert. He wants to know what in hell you're doing out of your jurisdiction, and for me to tell you to get the hell home."

"A continuing family squabble," Rocco said.

"That's your problem. Now, what's this crap about Haney and the Llewyn murder?"

"Suspicion only."

"Tell me a little B and E, tell me suspicion of rape or a little mugging, but Haney and murder—political murder—that's shit."

"Perhaps for hire," Lyon suggested.

Murdock glared and then leaned back in his creaking swivel chair. "Maybe. Junior could be hired to bludgeon his grandmother if it paid more than a sawbuck. What do you have on him?"

"Not much," Rocco said. "We traced everyone who was a registered motorcyclist and who purchased thirty-caliber ammo in the last week. It fits Junior. An hour ago we interviewed Loyce Haney. When we went to see Junior—"

"He'd skipped."

"Right. Of course he doesn't know why we want to talk to him."

"Knowing Junior, he's probably done something, and cops nosing around is all he needs to hear."

"You sound like you know him well," Lyon said.

Murdock squinted ominously. "Junior's twenty-eight. He's been known to this department since he was twelve. One of our more outstanding citizens. Started by stealing bicycles, advanced to cars—you name it. His sheet doesn't show half of what we've brought him in for."

"Political murder is slightly different than ripping off a Thunderbird."

Murdock's eyes glinted at them as he pulled a long cigar from a center desk drawer and lit it with a kitchen match. "Depends," he said in a noncommittal voice.

"You don't mean that," Rocco said.

Murdock's cigar went out and he lit it again, flipping the match toward an overflowing wastebasket. " 'Course not, Chief Herbert. I don't believe half I say and hardly anything I hear. Now, as far as politics and Junior are concerned—he can hardly read. Not that that stops some of them over in the state capitol. For money now . . . maybe."

"Would he kill?" Lyon asked.

Murdock contemplated the spiraling cloud of cigar smoke and made a lazy gesture with a finger through a smoke ring. "Well now, if I was in a position to want to eliminate someone . . . Junior would be available for a price."

"You think he's done it before?"

Murdock wrinkled his nose at Lyon. "If he'd done it before he wouldn't be here. I would have seen to that. I just said he would be available if approached."

"What about pulling a Lee Oswald?" Rocco asked.

"Junior's not nuts. He's what your do-gooders like Llewyn would have called underprivileged.

Translated to ordinary English, he's hungry as hell for what he can get."

The phone rang. Murdock closed a pudgy fist over the receiver and picked it up. He mumbled twice and slammed it back on the cradle. "A unit has located Junior's bike outside the Krauts' clubhouse."

"Junior?" Rocco asked.

Murdock stood up. "Hell, how would I know? I wouldn't let two of my men go into that place alone. That'd be like feeding them to the sharks. Come on, I'm taking a double backup crew down there to raid the joint."

The Krauts' M.C. clubhouse was located on Route 92 on the outskirts of Breeland. Three years earlier the peeling frame building had been an inn, with rooms for rent upstairs, and a small bar and grill on the first floor. The property had been condemned for a highway widening and was slated for destruction later in the year. In the interim, the Krauts had taken occupancy. Its windows were mostly shuttered, and a half dozen Harleys were neatly aligned in the overgrown parking lot.

Seven police cars with twice as many uniformed officers had formed a circle around the building. Murdock stood with a bullhorn near the wooden steps leading to the front door as Rocco swerved his cruiser to a stop near the side of the building.

"This is Captain Murdock. We're coming in and don't want trouble. All you in there, against the wall and take the position. I'm coming in on five. One . . ."

"I have the feeling they've been through this before," Lyon said.

"I hope they don't decide to relocate to Murphysville," Rocco replied.

". . . five. All right, here we come." Murdock, followed by several uniformed officers, clumped up the remaining steps and with a shattering kick opened the front door.

The splotched wooden bar was cluttered with empty beer cans. A man was stretched out on a cot in a far corner, and three other Krauts were playing pool on an ancient table. The police officers milled around the room as a pool player glanced uninterestedly in their direction and then back to the table to take his shot.

"I told you, against the wall," Murdock said to the pool player. "You hear me, Wiff?"

"I heard you, Captain. Get off our backs. We haven't done nothing. We got rights, you know."

Murdock stood directly in front of the club's leader, providing a sharp contrast to the tall, heavy-set man in the cut-off sweat shirt. "You shouldn't talk like that to the establishment, Wiff. It's not nice."

The captain's fist slammed into Wiff's solar plexus and knocked him back against the pool table. "Put 'em against the wall and see if they're clean," a police sergeant bellowed.

Wiff waved his pool cue toward Murdock. "I told you, Murdock. Lay off!"

"You want a trip downtown, Wiff?"

"Fuck you."

"I ought to bust your goddamn head."

"Come on, Fatso."

"Where's Junior Haney?"

"Don't know the gentleman."

"Take him," Murdock said to the waiting officers.

Six men hung back for a moment and then began to move in a tight semicircle toward Wiff. Wiff backed against the wall, the pool cue held to his front like a protecting lance.

"Take him now!" the sergeant yelled as they closed in on Wiff.

"Wait a goddamn minute," Rocco's voice echoed through the room and froze everyone. "He's mine." The chief moved through the attacking officers until he stood before Wiff with the tip of the pool cue an inch from his chest. "Take it easy, son," Rocco said in an even voice. "You and I are going to talk for a few minutes."

"Off you, pig."

"Now, now ." Rocco's mammoth hand closed over the pool cue, wrenched it effortlessly from Wiff's hand, and then snapped it in two. The two pieces fell to the floor with a clatter that sounded across the quiet room. Rocco stepped forward, placed both hands on Wiff's shoulders and turned him against the wall. He quickly and efficiently searched the leader of the bike gang, then turned Wiff back to face him. "Now, sit down," he said quietly.

Wiff backed toward a folding chair and plunked into it. He crossed his legs and glared up at Rocco. "All right, big mother fucker, what do you want?"

"I want to know where Junior Haney is, and I want to know right now."

"You may be a big bastard, but la ti da."

"You'll make me angry," Rocco replied evenly.

"The Krauts protect their own."

"You take the club up to Cape Cod a couple of times a summer, don't you?"

"So?"

"I'd like to know how you're going to get there without going through Murphysville. By way of Boston, maybe. It's only a hundred or so miles out of the way."

"You can't stop us."

"You know, I'm not even going to answer that."

"We got a right to go through Murphysville."

"Do you have any idea how many traffic violations I can stick on your club if I put my mind to it?"

"Junior's not here."

"His bike's outside."

"He came by earlier and wanted to sell it. Fizz bought it for a couple of yards."

"I'd call that a distress sale. That bike looks almost new."

"It is; he just bought it."

"Four thousand new?"

"Something like that."

"And yet he sold it for a couple of hundred?"

"He said he was hot. Had to get out of town."

"How'd he leave?"

"Thumbed it."

"How long ago?"

"Maybe half an hour."

"We'll pick him up," Murdock said. "He won't get far."

Rocco drummed his fingers impatiently on the steering wheel as they waited in the parking lot outside the Krauts' clubhouse. The Breeland police drove from the lot and headed in various directions as the Krauts moved insolently from the building and began to start their Harleys.

Conformity against conformity, Lyon thought. The departing Krauts seemed alike: German helments, leather jackets, or shirts cut off at the shoulder. Massive and sullen men, they roared from the lot with a scream of rubber and turned onto the highway in a single file that headed toward a lemming-like destruction.

"Suppose we ought to go home," Rocco said. "I can check the school crossing guards."

"School's out. I think we ought to check on Loyce Haney again."

"Crud like Junior won't bother about his wife and child. He's off like a big-assed bird."

"I don't think so."

Rocco looked at Lyon and nodded. He threw the car into gear.

As they stopped at the apartment on Halliburton Court, Lyon saw a curtain flutter at the window. Rocco knocked again and again; no answer. He increased the pressure of his pounding until he shook the wood of the door.

"Wait," Lyon said and put his hand over Rocco's fist. "Mrs. Haney, it's Lyon Wentworth. We must talk to you. I can't tell you how important it is. It's a question of Junior's safety."

There was silence from the apartment interior, and then the door opened a crack. The young woman's opaque eyes looked through the slim opening. "I don't know where Junior is. Please leave me alone."

"Junior will be dead in hours unless you let us help," Lyon said softly.

"He can take care of himself."

"Hear me out, Mrs. Haney. May I call you Loyce?"

"I suppose."

Lyon pushed on the door in a slow but persistent movement until it swung backward, and they stepped into the small apartment. Loyce Haney had changed into a blouse and skirt. The baby, still in the playpen, now wore a blue knit suit. He seemed puzzled by the whole affair. Past the kitchen area they could see into the bedroom. There was an open suitcase on the bed.

"What about Junior?" Loyce asked, and then seeing their gaze toward the suitcase quickly said, "If

Junior's in trouble again, I'm leaving. I told him that if he did anything again, I would."

"He called you?"

"I don't know where he is."

Lyon reached for her hand. Puzzled, she put it in his and he led her toward the couch, where they sat down together. Lyon turned toward her and spoke in a gentle voice. "You must trust me, Loyce."

"I—I don't know what's going on."

"I think I do, and therefore it's terribly important that you listen carefully."

"All right." Her voice was low, almost plaintive.

"Junior's involved in something with people he can't control. They paid him a good deal of money before the fact, twenty-five hundred, five thousand, and they promised him more."

She nodded.

"As soon as we left here earlier, you called Junior and told him of our visit. He left the station, sold his bike for a ridiculous amount of money, and has gone somewhere. Somewhere nearby and called you, told you to pack, that someone would come for you and take you to him, and then the three of you would go off. But it won't work that way. You must know that; they won't let him leave. They won't let you go with him. They are going to kill him, Loyce. I promise you that. He's been in contact with them, and they will not allow him to live."

She took her hand from Lyon's and pressed it against her cheek as her eyes stared into his. "Junior's not a bad guy, he really isn't."

"He's in well over his head this time. Tell us where he is."

"He . . . he called me."

"I know he did. From where?"

"I'm to meet him. He said a friend will give him money."

"Where?" Lyon asked softly.

"In—in a bar. Al's Place in Cyprus."

Lyon looked quickly toward Rocco, who was standing by the door. "About a ten-minute ride from here. We had better take her with us this time."

Al's Place was scrunched between two small factories. Its front windows were almost gray with grime, and the neon beer signs cast strange patterns through the dirty glass. Rocco parked the car down the street, away from the sight lines from the bar's interior.

Loyce Haney, holding her baby, huddled in the rear seat as Lyon turned toward her. "Do you have a snapshot of Junior?"

She pulled a small red wallet from her purse and handed it to Lyon. He unsnapped the clasp and flipped through the acetate photo covers until he came to one of a man astride a motorcycle. He held it up and she nodded.

"Let's go," Rocco said after glancing at the snapshot.

In the bar's dim interior two old men huddled over short beers and stared blankly at the game show on the wall television set. The bartender looked at the newcomers expectantly and took his elbows off the bar. As their eyes adjusted to the dim light, they could see a small back room with high-backed booths.

Junior Haney sat in the last booth and faced the door. His bottle of beer lay on its side and slowly rocked back and forth on the uneven table, dribbling small gushes of foam across the booth. As they walked toward him, his hands gripped the edge of the table, and he looked at them with blank eyes.

As Rocco strode ahead and put his hand on his shoulder, Junior slipped sideways until his head thunked against the wall. This movement revealed the knife hilt protruding from his abdomen.

"Rainbow," Junior mumbled as blood frothed from his mouth.

5

"He's dead," Rocco said as he slipped the service revolver from its holster, sprang toward the rear doors and disappeared outside.

"What the hell's going on here?" The bartender stood at the entrance to the back room, glaring at Lyon.

"Who or what is Rainbow?" Lyon snapped.

"What in hell you talking about? What's with the guy in the booth?"

"Who was back here? A few minutes ago, who was back here with him?"

"He looks sick or something."

"Answer my question, damn it!"

"I don't know. I didn't see nobody. Sometimes guys come in the back door."

Rocco came through the front door, still holding the revolver. "The streets and alleys are deserted. We must have missed him by minutes." He went behind the bar and began to dial the phone rapidly. "I'm calling the locals."

"Hey, that phone is private," the bartender said.

"You didn't see anyone with that man in the booth?"

"I told the other guy, no. Hey, this guy is dead."

"Yes," Lyon replied. "He's dead." He walked from the bar and down the street toward the cruiser. Loyce Haney looked up at him with wide eyes.

"Too late?" she asked.

"I'm sorry."

In the subdued senate chamber with its semicircle of mahogany desks, Senator Norton, from a district along the shore, was giving an interminable speech about the need for protection of the state's few remaining lobster beds. For the first time, Bea Wentworth found herself impatient with an ecological problem. She didn't really give a damn; she was too worried. Possessing one distinct advantage over the other thirty-five state senators, she reached up to her ear and turned off the hearing aid.

A few minutes earlier they had taken the first vote on her gun-legislation rider: ten for, nineteen against, four voting present and three absent. The speaking senator's voice had faded to an indistinct hum, a true blessing, and she tried to concentrate on a list of votes for the gun bill that might allow a solution for carrying it.

She found it difficult even to concentrate on her own bill. Her palms were perspiring; her heartbeat had increased. She knew she was suffering from anxiety. How did national leaders, some who seemed to exist under the daily threat of assassination, continue to function with any degree of efficiency? She was safe here—the sergeant-at-arms at the door, state police throughout the building, her own private cop by the grace of Rocco Herbert. She had nothing to worry about; she must put fear aside.

The hand on her shoulder made her start and almost fall from the seat.

A folded note was discreetly placed beside her arm.

IN THE HALL. WHEN YOU'RE FREE. LYON.

Bea slipped from her desk, crossed the carpeting of the sedate senate chamber and went into the baroque corridor. Lyon was leaning against a marble pillar midway down the hall. She walked toward him with a smile, waving at the young Murphysville police officer who was flirting with the coffee-wagon girl.

Lyon kissed Bea and held her hand as the police officer moved to her side. The three of them stood as a triumvirate at the balustrade under the dome.

"Lyon, this is Patrolman Jamie Martin. Rocco has asked him to accompany me."

"How are you?" Lyon asked and shook the young officer's hand. Oh, Lord, he thought. His wife protected by an adolescent with six weeks' experience. If anything happened, they'd be lucky if he didn't shoot himself in the foot—that is, if Rocco had let him have bullets for his gun.

"Fine, sir. I want you to know that I'm looking after Mrs. Wentworth real good."

"That's fine," Lyon said. "But I'd like to talk to my wife. Shouldn't you be looking for killers or something?"

The officer looked embarrassed and stepped back. "Of course." He walked a few feet away and began to peer suspiciously around the marble hallway.

"Somehow Jamie Martin doesn't give me a real sense of security," Bea said.

"I suppose it's the best Rocco could do. How many men can you yank off traffic duty?"

"Did you have any luck? This not knowing is driving me up a wall."

"We found him."

"Oh, Lyon, that's great. Who is he?"

"A fellow named Junior Haney, like the computer indicated. Just a young hood."

"Why me? What did he say?"

"Well, he didn't exactly say very much."

"I can't tell you how much better I feel. Do you have enough for Rocco to arrest him?"

"We've traced a rental van to him and a borrowed trail bike. Rocco's making a cast of the trail bike tires now; at first glance they seem to resemble the tire prints found behind the church."

"Then it definitely is him?"

"Yes."

"But he won't say anything?"

Lyon took his wife's arm. "He said something. Let's get a cup of coffee."

"WHO THE HELL IS RAINBOW? WHAT IS RAINBOW?" Bea spilled coffee as she leaned across the small cafeteria table.

"We don't know."

"His wife must know something."

"They've been interrogating her for hours. She doesn't seem to know anything more than the fact that her husband came into money. Junior spent a great deal of time away from home, either at his motorcycle club, or just out and about. We've also found out that he took time off from work the day of the murder."

"Then he was obviously hired by this Rainbow."

"Yes. Will you have sugar, Officer Martin?"

"Right."

"Oh, Lord. Here comes you know who," Bea said.

They all turned to see Senator Mackay approaching their table with a wide smile. He gave a perfunctory wave to Lyon and sat in a chair close to Bea.

"They told me you'd be here, Senator Wentworth."

"I have enemies everywhere."

"There's still time for us to get together before the convention."

"A rather close but reliable source informs me that your feelings can be summed up by 'That broad's got to go.' "

"A figure of speech, Senator. Many diverse political animals have learned to cooperate."

Bea leaned forward and spoke in a low and intense voice. "Ted, I enjoy politics, but if I were defeated tomorrow, my life would not come to an end. And if it meant my defeat, I would not vote for you or encourage others to vote for you. We need men of vision, not opportunists."

Ted Mackay stood and smiled fixedly down at Bea. "Senator Wentworth, you're going to regret that."

"Is that a threat?"

"Take it as you will."

Ted Mackay strode from the small cafeteria, his body turning from side to side as he waved at other diners.

Lyon stood at the kitchen window and looked toward the rear of the house, where a police officer, a rifle cradled in his arms, walked slowly back and forth along the patio. He shook his head sadly.

"What's the matter?" Bea asked from the cutting board next to the stove.

"It's a hell of a way to live—guards at the door, a pistol in the desk."

"I feel better with them out there."

"I suppose." He kept to himself the knowledge that Rocco could maintain the guards for only another seven days, that already he was under pressure from the board of selectmen over the cost. One of the members of the board, who discounted any conspiratorial theories of assassination, insisted that it was all a waste of time. Lyon knew that Rocco had squeezed the additional week only by threatening to resign.

"You know, Lyon," Bea said as she pointed a cucumber at him, "when this whole thing started, Rocco talked of our making a list of enemies."

"It wouldn't hurt."

"There's one man in this state who would head both our lists, one man who stood to gain the most if Llewyn and I were both dead."

"Ted Mackay."

"He's ambitious enough, ruthlessly so . . . although I can't conceive of Ted's pulling the trigger."

"Junior was paid to pull the trigger."

"It amounts to the same thing."

"It might in your mind, but not in others'. Removal from the deed seems to salve certain consciences."

Her knife cut vehemently across the cucumber as pieces fell rapidly into the salad bowl. "If it's not Ted, we'd have to assume that Junior was one of those outsiders, like most assassins. One of those skewed, unhappy, screwed-up people . . ."

"He didn't put a knife into his own stomach."

Bea looked at the knife she was holding. "I guess you're right." Absently, she began to toss the salad. "I forgot the tomatoes." She crossed to the sink with a tomato in each hand, gave Lyon a playful poke in the side with her elbow, and began to run water over the vegetables.

Rocco Herbert's daughter, Remley, had brought the tomatoes over yesterday, and Lyon wondered how it was that Rocco always had the earliest tomatoes of the season.

A hole surrounded by a spidery web of cracked glass appeared in the top pane of the window over the sink. Bea turned toward Lyon with a look of bewilderment.

He stepped toward her. His movements in the still air seemed slow, tenuous, as if a dozen years elapsed while he traversed the five steps across the kitchen floor.

A second hole appeared in the lower left quadrant of the window. A buzzing whir tore through the lower portion of his shirt sleeve. The kitchen clock on the far wall shattered as plaster dust spun through the room.

Lyon lunged the final step, grasped Bea around the waist and, as they fell, twisted so that his body covered hers.

A third shot pierced the window and ricocheted off the molding. He felt Bea squirm beneath him as he tried to count. "One thousand." The distant sounds of the rifle shots echoed from the surrounding hills. It must have taken him a second to fling himself at Bea and fall to the floor, a total of two seconds. He tried to remember: muzzle velocity and the decrease of velocity over hundred-meter intervals. Two seconds, high muzzle velocity from a powerful rifle. He estimated speed at impact at 2,000 feet per second, perhaps a 3,200- or 3,500-feet-per-second muzzle velocity.

The rifleman would be across the river in the cliffs along the far bank.

Firing began from the patio outside the window. Jamie Martin was returning the shots.

Lyon ran for the door and rushed out to the patio, where the young officer was kneeling by the parapet, firing across the river.

"No, Jamie!" Lyon yelled.

"I saw a muzzle flash, Mr. Wentworth."

"Stop it!" Lyon reached over and pulled the rifle from the officer's grasp. "He could be anywhere over there. You want to kill some Boy Scouts?"

"I saw a flash."

"The secret, Mr. Wentworth, is to let the shadow of the vermouth bottle fall across the gin." Danny Nemo gently stirred the martini pitcher at the small bar in the corner of Dawkins's Castle's living room.

"They look too good to pass up, Danny. Belay the sherry." Lyon swiveled on the bar stool to look toward the fireplace, where Bea was talking animatedly with Wilkie Dawkins. Rocco Herbert left the group and crossed to Lyon.

"When is this joker supposed to show up?"

"Senator Mackay told me when I phoned that he'd be here by seven," Danny Nemo replied.

"It's five past now."

"I'm sure he'll be here shortly." With a professional twist, Danny poured cocktails from the glass pitcher. As if sensing the completion of the bartending, Wilkie Dawkins and Bea came toward the bar.

"Superb as usual," Wilkie said as he sipped his drink.

"I keep in practice, Captain."

"How long till your leave, Danny?" Wilkie asked.

"Another ten days, sir."

"Leave?" Lyon asked.

"Right," Wilkie replied. "Fifty weeks a year Danny is my legs, bartender and secretary. Two weeks a year he goes gambling and blows a year's salary on the tables. Last year Monte Carlo, this year Vegas."

"That's a leave for an ex-tennis player army non-com, Mr. Wentworth," Danny said.

"Do you ever win?" Bea asked.

"Anything I win the broads seem to get."

"I usually wire him the return fare," Wilkie said.

"Are you sure Mackay is coming?"

"He damn well better," Dawkins replied. "I'm still his biggest contributor, and I carry a little weight on the state committee."

"I appreciate your help," Lyon said.

"It's not really help. I want this whole matter cleared up. No accusations or innuendoes."

"We haven't made any accusations."

"Someone shot at you today and you want to talk to Ted—I call that an innuendo."

"He wasn't very cooperative when I called him; that's why I came to you."

"I think there's some sort of radical group involved here that has nothing to do with Ted." Danny Nemo refilled their glasses as Wilkie pushed his wheelchair back from the group. "A hard-core dozen is all they'd need. Good Lord, how many did Castro have when he started? Hitler? Mao had six in his group during the early twenties."

"I hardly think that whoever's behind this can be classified in that category," Bea said.

"Why not? So this group is at the far right of the spectrum instead of the far left. I've often suspected that the spectrum was circular anyway."

As the argument continued, Lyon tapped Rocco on the shoulder and motioned him to a corner of the living room. "What's the report on the tire prints?"

"Positive. The front tire of the trail bike Junior borrowed is a positive match with the cast we made at the church by the green."

"Anything on who or what Rainbow is?"

"Not a damn thing. I've run it past all the agencies, here and in Washington. Negative all the way."

"Have the Breeland or state police come up with anything?"

"Blank everywhere."

The faint echo of door chimes seeped through the room, and Danny Nemo moved unobtrusively toward the hall. Conversation died out as Wilkie swiveled his wheelchair to face the door as everyone waited expectantly.

Ted Mackay entered the room as he always did—with a broad smile and a wave. Then, with both arms extended, he crossed to Bea and kissed her on the forehead. Startled, she took a backward step.

The majority leader swept through the room. Lyon received a hearty handshake, Rocco a pat on the shoulder, and Wilkie Dawkins a double handshake. Mackay ended at the bar, where he picked up the cocktail glass Danny had conveniently filled. He raised it in the air.

"I don't know what's responsible for this—Lyon's good offices with his wife, Wilkie and his sometimes not so subtle political pressure, or Bea's own inimitable method of decision making; but, nevertheless, I propose a toast to Bea Wentworth, the next lieutenant governor of this state."

Bea's glass slipped from her fingers to shatter on the hearth. "I'm sorry," she said. "I'm afraid I don't understand."

"You've obviously decided to back my nomination, and I can't think of anyone else I'd rather have on the ticket with me." Ted's eyebrow rose above his smile as he looked from one to another. "Isn't that why Wilkie insisted I meet with you?"

Wilkie cleared his throat. "I'm afraid not, Ted."

Ted Mackay took a sip of his drink. "My apologies. I was obviously premature. I'm sure there are details to work out before the final commitment of support."

"I didn't come here tonight to throw you my support, Ted," Bea said, and then mumbled to Lyon under her breath, "and that's the understatement of the year."

"What did you say?"

"I'm concerned over the threat you made in the cafeteria today."

Mackay laughed. "You don't mean the 'You'll regret that' bit?"

"I certainly do."

"My apologies, Senator Wentworth. I didn't realize your political skin was so thin."

"It's not my political skin I'm worried about."

"I'm afraid I'm not following the thrust of this conversation," Ted said to Wilkie. "Can you clarify things for me?"

"There was an attempt on Bea's life earlier today. We felt you should be informed."

Ted handed his glass to Danny for a refill and

looked thoughtful. "You think some sort of conspiracy is trying to eliminate party leadership?"

"It's possible," Lyon said. "Llewyn has been killed, and now there have been two attempts on Bea's life. We can't come up with any possible motive except political."

Mackay tapped his fingers on the edge of the bar. "Well, I have to confess I'm disappointed. I expected to come here for a finalization of political support, and instead I find we're all playing amateur detective."

"It was hardly an amateur who shot through my kitchen window," Bea said.

"I've always known you had far-out opinions," Ted said to Bea. "Now I find out that you're one of those nuts who thinks all killings are political murders, with the CIA or the commies lurking in the brush."

"I don't think someone shot through my window. I know."

Ted Mackay threw up his arms in mock resignation. "All right, I'll play. We'll have a brain-storming session on who killed Randy Llewyn."

"If you have any ideas or even conjectures, Ted, I think at this point they would be greatly appreciated," Wilkie said.

"Conjecture is too honorable a word. How about a wild guess?"

"Try us," Bea said.

"All right. I have the feeling there's an ultra-right-wing radical group involved here. Randy Llewyn was a liberal. Verged on the socialist, if you ask me; and I think certain elements wanted him removed."

"And me also?" Bea asked.

"Yes."

Wilkie nodded his head in agreement. "We discussed this earlier, Ted, and I tend to agree with you. The whole situation smacks of conspiracy."

Bea looked thoughtful. "I'm sorry. I don't buy it. One of us, or someone in a governmental agency, would have had some information on the existence of such a group."

"I said it was a wild guess," Ted responded. "It's far more plausible than the unspoken thought in this room that I'm behind this."

"We don't even suggest that," Lyon said.

"You don't have to. It's written all over you."

"You ever hear of Rainbow?" Rocco asked.

"Rainbow what?"

"The name. Does it mean anything to you?"

"I think I once had dinner at a place called the Rainbow Room."

"That's all?"

The Mackay smile reappeared and focused on Wilkie Dawkins. "You know, Wilkie, if I didn't know better, I'd say this was becoming an inquisition."

"I think everyone here is trying to clear the air, Ted," Wilkie said. "When you analyze the situation, and I think this may be lurking in the back of certain people's minds, you would benefit if Llewyn and Bea were both . . . gone."

"You know, I'd laugh if this weren't so serious."

Wilkie swiveled his chair to face Rocco. "I agree with Ted. I'm sure that he is not a suspect in a murder investigation. I for one happen to know that he spent the day in his campaign headquarters surrounded by a dozen people."

"I never made an accusation," Rocco said. "Let's say we're involved in a routine inquiry."

Wilkie rolled his chair several paces closer to

Rocco. "And let's keep it that way, Chief Herbert. The slightest innuendo against a respected member of the legislature is hardly routine."

"That was a waste of time," Lyon said as he drove back to their house.

"I still think Mackay is involved," Bea said. "I'm sure he's perfectly capable of having engineered this whole thing. There's an opportunistic quality in him that frightens me."

"I can see his possible motive, but you—"

"Can't take a man to court on motive alone."

The road curved in a parallel course along the river, and Lyon drove slowly and carefully as Bea leaned against his shoulder. The full moon appeared intermittently through the trees, and in the rear-view mirror he could see Rocco's cruiser behind them.

"Rainbow. Who is Rainbow?" Bea asked in a singsong. "Maybe we'll get lucky, like Dorothy, and find out who the wizard really is."

"What's that?" Lyon asked, but Bea had closed her eyes and burrowed deeper against his jacket.

They had tried talking to Mackay and gotten nowhere. The answer was in the identification of Rainbow, and the only way to effect that would be through the trail leading from Junior Haney. Tomorrow Lyon would start on the re-creation of Junior Haney's life.

6

Fzzt! Fzzt!

Beer tab tops flipped across the room. The case of Bud that Lyon had brought was rapidly dwindling. Half a dozen pairs of hands reached into the case of beer, shook cans, ripped off tabs with a flourish, and spurted beer toward the ceiling.

Beer spewed past his ear as someone cackled. Lyon sat on the edge of the pool table in the Krauts M.C. clubhouse. Wiff Stamen, wearing a sweat shirt with the legend "Feerlus Leader," straddled a straight chair immediately in front of him.

Fizz Nichols lay on his back with his head propped on a World War I German helmet and let beer trickle into his mouth. Other members of the club sat around the room in varying poses and degrees of hostility.

It was the one in the corner whacking the tire chain into his palm whom Lyon found the most unsettling.

"I want to write a fair article about you guys for the Sunday supplement," Lyon said. "An article showing that a motorcycle club is interested in more than rape, plunder and pillage."

There was ominous silence from the group. Fizz Nichols drained half his can of beer and belched.

"What's pillage?" Wiff Stamen asked.

"Looting."

"Like ripping off stuff?"

"That's the basic idea."

Two crushed beer cans cartwheeled past Lyon's head and fell behind the ancient bar, where they clunked against their predecessors. Full cans were flipped around the room, tabs were torn off, and several streams of beer crisscrossed the room.

Wiff sipped his beer and contemplated the foam for a moment. "You better take a different approach, like maybe bike safety."

"Come on, Wiff," Fizz Nichols said. "Sure, we done a little pillaging, but no rapes—well, not for a long time."

"What's your angle, Wentworth?"

Lyon knew damn well that his angle was a complete re-creation of Junior Haney's life in the hope that some clue or lead toward Rainbow would be discovered. But revealing that to the assembled group would be an invitation to a stomping. "An article. I feel that motorcyclists have been maligned."

"Yeah, they bust us a lot," a voice said as several others nodded in assent.

"You written something before?"

"Yes, several books."

"Like what?"

At this point Lyon needed a beer. He opened a can before replying. "Well, my most successful was *The Monster on the Mantel*, and *The Cat in the Capital* hasn't done badly."

"You've got to be kidding."

"I try to be versatile."

"What do we get out of this?"

"I buy the beer."

"And you want to ride with us?"

"Do whatever you guys do."

"We'll take a vote," Wiff said.

"How much beer?" Fizz asked.

The vote was taken while Lyon made a quick trip to the nearest liquor store for three additional cases of beer. On his return, he found that he had been officially elected a temporary probationary member of the Krauts, but of course not entitled to wear colors.

Since Lyon had only $63.50 in cash, and the members refused to take a check, the poker game was over in an hour. Three other members, back from the night shift at a local factory, joined the group and aided in the demise of the remaining beer.

After he raked in the last poker pot, consisting mostly of Lyon's money, Fizz Nichols got unsteadily to his feet. "All right, let's ride. Man, let's scratch rubber and roar!"

"Get Wentworth a hog," Wiff ordered.

"I'm not really hungry," Lyon replied.

"Oh, Jesus," voices said simultaneously.

They borrowed a hog from one of the members who was entertaining his old lady in an upper room. It was the largest motorcycle Lyon had ever seen: 1200-cc displacement, factory outfitted, sheepskin seat, curved windshield and metal saddlebags. He approached the monolithic machine with trepidation.

"Watch for the suicide clutch," Wiff whispered in his ear as the club mounted up.

"What's that?"

"Don't kick off until you want to go; otherwise the hog goes without you."

"Move out!"

They rode two abreast, with Fizz and Wiff in the lead. Traffic gave them a wide berth, and Lyon felt as if they were playing the adolescent game of King of the Hill. In downtown Breeland they made two circles around the town square and headed out Cumberland Street. As they approached the Exxon station where Junior Haney had been employed, Lyon revved his engine, held up his hand and pointed to his gas tank.

The cycles made a loop into the gasoline station and stopped on the tarmac near the pumps. Junior's replacement, an acned man in dirty jeans, shuffled over to Lyon. Because of the huge consumption of beer, the remainder of the club lined up outside restrooms, disregarding the sex differentiation signs on the doors.

"Fill it up," Lyon said and climbed off the motorcycle. "Rainbow been around?"

"Huh?"

"I heard Rainbow was coming around."

"I don't know what you're talking about, mister, and this hog is only taking a gallon."

As Lyon borrowed sixty-three cents from Fizz to pay the attendant for his gallon of gasoline, three City of Breeland patrol cars swerved into the station. Two cars blocked the station entrance, while the third swiveled to a stop near Lyon at the pump island.

Captain Sean Murdock grunted his way from the third car as the Krauts lined up around Lyon.

"Why the hassle, Murdock?" Wiff asked.

"No safety helmets. We're writing you all up for violation of the helmet law."

"Off our backs!" Fizz yelled.

"Shuddup and pull out your licenses and registrations. You, with the sneakers and no socks, over here."

"Me?" Lyon asked.

"Yes, you. What're you doing playing with the kiddies? Over here, fast!"

Lyon fumbled for his wallet as he walked slowly toward Captain Murdock. Murdock grabbed him by the shoulders and pulled him around the car.

"What in hell are you doing, Wentworth?"

"Riding with the club."

"What kind of crap is that?"

"I thought I might learn something."

"Get back to Murphysville, where you belong. Where's Herbert?"

"Following another lead."

"I don't like amateurs fooling around in my town."

"I'm doing an article on the club."

"Bull crap! I'm taking you back to your car and escorting you out of Breeland."

"I'm not through here, Captain."

"Stubborn bastard, aren't you?" With his pinkie, Murdock signaled to his car's driver. "Write this guy up."

"What for, Captain?"

"Violation of the helmet law, driving without a motorcycle operator's permit, lack of registration."

"Wait a minute, Murdock."

"Resisting arrest and breach of peace."

"Hey!"

"Cuff him."

With the exception of the time that Rocco Herbert's wife had kicked the poker club out of the house and they had adjourned to the Murphysville jail for completion of the game, this was the only time Lyon had been in a jail cell. He didn't like it. Nine feet long and six wide. He paced angrily until reminded of a large leopard incarcerated in a zoo. He smiled. *The Cheetah and the Cell*—it might work. He sat back in the bunk and put his hands behind his head and began to think about the large cat with the streamlined musculature, held imprisoned, all the while yearning. . . .

The clank of metal on metal awakened him, and he sat up to see Rocco Herbert in the corridor outside the cell. The chief's fingers curled over the bar as he looked at Lyon sardonically.

"Resisting arrest. Jesus Christ, Lyon."

"Damn it all, Rocco, I didn't do anything."

"Captain Murdock says you did."

Murdock appeared behind Rocco to unlock the barred door. "I didn't book him. But get him out of town. He's a troublemaker."

Lyon and Rocco walked out of the Breeland police station into a bright afternoon sun. Lyon squinted a moment until his eyes adjusted to the light. As they walked to the Murphysville police cruiser, Lyon turned to Rocco.

"I thought Murdock was a little overzealous."

"What do you mean by that?"

"His insistence that I was meddling."

"Are you trying to suggest that he's somehow mixed up in this? That's paranoid, Lyon. That's paranoid as hell."

"Maybe. I'm getting suspicious of everyone at this point. You come up with anything?"

"Nothing. Come on, I'll drive you to your car."

"Leave me at the clubhouse."

"Your car."

"Like I said, the clubhouse."

In honor of Lyon's bust, Wiff and Fizz called another club for a protest ride-in to the state capitol. The very mention of the helmet law made the bikers shake with anger, and voices and yells crossed the clubhouse parking lot as two dozen motorcycles revved engines in preparation for the start. Lyon had again been loaned the large Harley and given a position of honor immediately behind Wiff Stamen.

The onslaught of the long line of motorcycles had obviously been called ahead by the state police. As they approached the gold-domed state capitol, they saw that barriers had been erected, and a dozen state police were positioned around the circular drive.

The officers, in wide-brimmed hats, directed the cyclists and allowed them to park directly in front of the building. Over the months of helmet protests, a code of unwritten laws had sprung up. The police, on their part, would not issue summonses to the bikers while they were protesting, if the bikers followed directions for parking, stayed off the grass, and were moderately well behaved.

The club members began to chant; signs appeared. As Lyon, with a sore rump, climbed off the Harley, he wished he could ride back in an automobile.

"WENTWORTH, WHAT IN HELL ARE YOU DOING?"

He looked up to see Bea leaning from an upstairs window. "Protesting."

She shook her head.

State police impassively lined the steps under the glinting dome. After the obligatory circling of the drive combined with a crescendo of revving engines, the bikers formed a phalanx of machines by the steps and began to chant. After a little difficulty, Lyon managed to align himself next to Wiff Stamen. "What now?"

"Not much. We make noise for a while, and then they let one of us go inside to present our demands to a politico."

"What are our demands?"

"No helmets, stop the harassment, anything we can think of."

"Sounds fine," Lyon replied as the sound of engines drowned out his voice.

Captain Norbert of the state police walked slowly down the capitol steps and glared at the impatient riders. He tilted his hat over his eyes, folded his arms across his chest, and walked slowly across the driveway. Bikes swerved out of his path in order to avoid hitting him, and he continued his slow progress as if oblivious of the motorcycles buzzing on either side. When he reached the end of the drive, he held up a hand and the moving bikes formed a semicircle around him.

"One guy and one guy alone can make a presentation to Senator Mackay."

"The hell with him. We want the governor."

"The governor's not here today. Mackay is all you get."

"Who's going in?"

"Send the writer in; he can speak good."

Hands pulled at Lyon and pushed him in front of Captain Norbert. The state police captain glared at him. "What in hell are you doing here, Wentworth?"

"Afternoon, Captain. I have been chosen to represent the Angels and the Krauts in order to make a formal protest to the State of Connecticut."

"Follow me." Lyon followed Norbert back across the drive, up the capitol steps, and down a marble hall. "You know, Wentworth, I always knew my brother-in-law had crazy buddies, but you win hands down."

"Doing my thing, Captain."

They stopped at the senate majority leader's office. Captain Norbert stepped aside as Lyon entered the office and walked toward Ted Mackay's desk.

Surprised, Mackay looked up and extended a hand. "Hello, Lyon. If you're here about the altercation, I'm sure we can work something out."

"I am here on behalf of the Krauts and the Angels."

"Sit down."

"Consider that I have formally protested the state's helmet law."

"You have done so."

"Is that right, Senator Mackay?"

The clubhouse floor had begun to tilt. In some dim recess of the frame building someone retched. The Breeland supermarket had been pleased to accept Lyon's check for several additional cases of beer—and almost the full complement of the club had aided in the task of finishing every can. Lyon felt bloated and knew he was half-smashed on the infinite number of beers he had consumed.

"You did fine, Wentworth," Wiff said from his prone position on the floor. Turning, he tilted the dregs of a can into his mouth and gave Lyon a wide, sloppy grin. "Just fine. We might even make you official."

"Mackay didn't say much."

"Didn't hardly say a word to Junior."

Something had just passed—a lead, and he strained to grasp it. He put both feet firmly on the floor, and the room began to steady. "Junior Haney? The one who was killed?"

"Yeah, he went in last time. He saw Mackay but didn't get nowhere. Junior never got nowhere except dead."

"They say Rainbow killed him."

"That's what the cops kept asking when they pulled us in. You're all right, Wentworth. You know that?—you're all right."

"You wouldn't tell them about Rainbow?"

"I don't know nothing to tell."

Lyon tried to think about that. He wanted to close his eyes and sleep under the pool table—but he couldn't do that, because Fizz Nichols was already curled up under the pool table. He fought for control and sobriety. It wasn't only the beer—a couple of members had brought bottles of rye, and the drinking had really become serious at ten when Wiff insisted that everyone drink boilermakers . . . a shot and a beer . . . a shot and a beer . . . it seemed to go on endlessly.

What time was it? It was late, and most of the club had either left or were asleep in various parts of the building. Only Wiff, curled near Lyon's feet, had any semblance of consciousness.

Lyon kicked Wiff in the side until he turned over.

"What?"

"He was wearing his colors when he was killed." That wasn't quite true, but it would do.

"What you talking about?"

"Junior Haney had his colors on when he was killed, and you guys don't give a damn. Let the cops bumble along, you just don't care that a Kraut was killed with his colors on."

"Like hell!" Wiff lumbered to his feet, lost his balance and caught the edge of the pool table. "We take care of our own."

"Not Junior."

"This Rainbow knocked him off?"

"That's what Junior said."

"We'll take care of the bastard. Can't kill a Kraut, especially when he's wearing colors."

"Someone knows about Rainbow?"

"That's what the cops kept asking."

"No club member would talk to a cop," Lyon said.

"Right." Wiff looked at Lyon with a dim recognition of what that meant. "I'm half-drunk."

"I think we all are."

"Okay, let's start."

Wiff led Lyon to a galvanized stall shower behind the barroom. The hot water didn't work, but the cold water was quite cold. Turning the nozzle on as far as it would go, Wiff stepped into the shower fully dressed and let the cold water run over his body. After five minutes he stepped out, bowed, and pointed to Lyon.

Lyon gasped as the water ran down the collar of his jacket and over his back. He bent his head back and let the cold spray play across his face. Finally, he felt Wiff tugging on his sleeve impatiently.

Wiff's interrogation of his fellow club members was direct, incisive and brutal. The preliminaries began with a bucket of cold water across the face, and a little face-slapping to catch their attention. A slam against the wall emphasized the immediate necessity for answers.

"You hear of Rainbow? Junior say anything to you?"

They proceeded to question all of the Krauts in the clubhouse. Fizz Nichols, placidly sleeping under the pool table, was the last. Lyon and Wiff each grabbed a foot and pulled him out onto the open floor, where Wiff applied water and slaps until he bent Fizz back over the pool table.

"Rainbow mean anything to you?"

"Leave me alone, mother fucker."

More slaps. "Rainbow?"

"Yeah, yeah. Now leave me alone, I'm tired."

"Who is he?"

Lyon found a small jar of instant coffee and a propane burner in a back room. He boiled water and made black coffee. When he returned to the barroom, Fizz was sitting on a straight chair with his head in his hands. He drank the coffee more out of fear than desire.

"Okay, buddy boy," Wiff said. "Junior was knocked off wearing colors. Wentworth here thinks some joker named Rainbow did it. Take it slow and easy, and tell us what you know."

"Quit leaning on me, man."

"Just tell us."

"Okay, okay. Some guy calling himself Rainbow telephoned Junior and asked if he wanted to make a few bucks. You know Junior; he was all for it. This guy wants Junior to meet him at a bar in Hartford for details . . . no names, nothing like that. Gave Junior a time, place, and booth in the bar. Junior asked me to go along, stay out of sight, follow the guy and act as backup, case things got rough."

"So, what happened?"

"I don't know. Nothing. Junior went to the place like he was told. I sat at the bar so I could have a look at the booth where he was to meet this guy. I carried a sock full o' bird shot, case Junior gave the high sign. This guy came in, sat with Junior twenty minutes, maybe half an hour."

"What did he look like?" Lyon asked.

"An ordinary working guy. Tan pants, windbreaker."

"Height, weight, color of hair?"

"Built like most guys, you know. Maybe thirty-five, brown hair—just a guy."

"Then what happened?"

"When he left, I tailed him, like Junior asked. He went to a fleabag hotel about six, seven blocks away and went up to a second-floor room in the front. I saw him in the window when he turned the light on. I go back to the bar where Junior is swattin' down brandy, like he was loaded, which he was. He slips me fifty and says he made his deal and to forget everything I saw."

"And you did?"

"Hell, yes. Like Junior was a fellow Kraut, right?"

"Yes, he was," Lyon said softly.

7

The early-morning sun was beginning to burn off the tendrils of fog rising from the river. The sun's rays rose over the hills and pierced the windshield of the small car. Lyon pulled down the sun visor and pinched the bridge of his nose to exorcise the massive headache. There is nothing worse than a beer hangover, he thought as he turned up the drive to Nutmeg Hill.

A young patrolman was leaning against a pine tree playing mumblety-peg in a patch of dirt. Lyon slowed the car to a halt. The officer looked up and smiled.

"Hi, Mr. Wentworth."

"Hello, Jamie. Everything quiet?"

"Yes, sir." Oh, Lord. The family homestead protected by an adolescent with six weeks' experience.

"Want some coffee?"

"Mrs. Wentworth gave me some a few minutes ago. She's in the back working in the garden."

Bea Wentworth, wearing shorts and a floppy shirt, was kneeling in the garden below the back patio. She carefully placed a plant in a small hole, watered it, pushed dirt around delicate stems and began to trim back leaves.

The sun, midway above the horizon, slanted through the oak tree to the side and speckled light across the side of her face, giving her a diffused, gentle appearance. Lyon felt that his wife was a woman of many seasons, a multifaceted person whose appearance and personality could change in the various life guises she chose. Now, kneeling on the warm earth and holding a small plant made her look as if she had been nurtured and had bloomed in the warming early day. At other times, like that day on the green when she introduced Llewyn, her outward appearance was forceful and charismatic.

And yet, the day on the green had shattered into a thousand shards when a rifle cracked from the church, and she had missed death by inches. On another day, in their own kitchen, a similar weapon had been fired from across the river.

He experienced a surge of feeling that made him want to reach toward her in an unseen grasp. He wanted to kneel in the dirt by her side and hold her. He knew his wife was independent, at times prepared to battle the world if necessary; and yet now he saw and loved another quality.

He bent over and kissed the back of her neck.

"OH, MY GOD!" Bea leaped to her feet with the trowel extended in a parrying position. When she saw who it was, her body sagged. "You scared the living daylights out of me."

"You looked so cute, I wanted to kiss you. Except now your knees are dirty, and what are you doing?"

"Propagating weeds."

"I thought weeds were capable of propagating themselves."

"KNOCK IT OFF, WENTWORTH. WHERE IN HELL WERE YOU LAST NIGHT?"

"Would you believe I was getting drunk with a motorcycle gang?"

"From you—yes. I am now the only member of the legislature whose spouse has protested the helmet law. I'll believe anything."

"Ted Mackay knew Junior Haney."

Bea placed her trowel on the patio and brushed her knees. "That doesn't make sense. I know he sometimes travels in strange company, but are you trying to tell me that the senate majority leader of this state was friends with a convicted felon who was a member of a motorbike gang?"

"I didn't say friends, only that he had met Junior and was alone with him for at least five minutes during the last helmet protest."

"Have you told Rocco?"

"Not yet. I'm going to phone him now." As they started for the house he put his arm around her.

"Lyon, I've heard about those bike gangs, and how they have old ladies or debs, or whatever they call them, and they all go . . . and did they, or did you, or . . ."

"No, but after I call Rocco—your weed propagation has given me a great idea."

He awoke to a heavy pounding on the door. "Who is it?"

"The man is downstairs and won't go away," Kim said from the hallway. "He says you two take an awful lot of naps."

Bea moaned deliciously and turned to Lyon. "What's up?"

"Rocco's downstairs."

"And pacing like a bear," Kim said. "But tell Bea to wash the dirt off her knees."

Rocco paced the long country-style kitchen as a glaring Kim sat on a stool with her arms akimbo.

"Damn it all, Kim. I haven't used a rubber hose in weeks."

"On the blacks or whites?"

"Only the blacks; the bruises don't show so easily."

"Comes the revolution, you're going to the wall—if we can find a wall high enough."

"Come on, you two," Lyon said as he poured coffee from the electric percolator.

They squeezed into the breakfast nook while Lyon, balancing his coffee cup, paced. He recounted the previous day's events. He started with the helmet protest and the fact that Mackay had met Junior Haney, and then continued with Fizz Nichols's admission that he had acted as backup during Junior's first meeting with Rainbow, and had in fact seen Rainbow and followed him back to the hotel.

"What are Fizz and Wiff doing now?" Rocco asked.

"They promised me that as soon as they were in shape they'd cruise Hartford to try to locate the hotel where Fizz trailed Rainbow. Then they'll call me."

Rocco drummed his fingers on the table as Kim stared icily at the thumping hand. "We have a motive for Mackay already, and now we have knowledge that

Mackay knew Rainbow. We could probably find witnesses to that effect."

"For the first time we have a living witness who actually saw Rainbow."

"Now that we know that Mackay and Rainbow are one and the same," Bea said.

"It's possible," Lyon replied. "It could be happenstance. After all, Mackay was the one the state police took me to see. Then again, it is a further step toward Mackay."

Rocco brought his fist down on the table. "Damn it all, I think Mackay is Rainbow! But how do we prove it? You say Fizz saw Rainbow?"

"It could be Mackay," Lyon responded. "Except for an age discrepancy. He says Rainbow is about thirty-five."

"But he saw him from a distance," Bea said. "A little hair dye, a change of clothes . . ."

"Could be," Lyon said. "Do we have any pictures of Ted in the house?"

It didn't take long for Bea to find several pictures of Mackay. Ted and Bea during the signing of a bill, Ted at a political rally. On the assumption that the shot that killed Llewyn and the one that missed Bea were politically motivated, Ted stood to gain the most, Lyon thought.

"Fizz thinks he can I-D Rainbow?" Rocco asked.

"He thinks maybe."

"Then we show him the photographs," Bea said.

"As soon as they call me," Lyon replied.

"He sure in hell has a motive," Rocco said. "That is if he wants the nomination bad enough to kill for it."

Lyon sat before his typewriter and bit a nail. The residue of the hangover was still sufficient to cast a dull film over his thought process, and his mind seemed to go in aimless patterns without coherence. How do you write for children about benign monsters when the true monsters of the world are sitting on your doorstep?

The phone rang. It was Rocco. "They've got your playmates in the Hartford jail," he said.

"What in hell for?"

"Do you want to make notes?"

"Come on, Rocco!"

"Two counts of breaking and entering, possession of an M-16, two live hand grenades and a loaded flare pistol."

"Oh, my God. They were going to kill Rainbow."

" 'Burn the mother fucker' is the exact quote."

Detective Sergeant Pat Pasquale was leaning against the wall outside his office. He put his thumb on his nose and waggled his fingers at Rocco.

"How's the angle of the dangle, Pasquale?" Rocco asked.

"Surviving, Rocco. Surviving. Do you know who I've got in my office? The beast has arrived."

"Captain Murdock?"

"None other. The civil libertarians' composite of police brutality."

"What's he doing here?"

"We called Breeland as a matter of courtesy when we picked up those two jokers. He was down here like a shot."

They crowded into Pasquale's small office, where Captain Murdock was already sitting with his heavy thighs straddling the small folding chair underneath a hovering cloud of cigar smoke. He waved the cigar at Rocco and Lyon as Pasquale sat down behind the desk.

"Now, will you all tell me what in hell is going on here?" Murdock rasped.

"I understand Pasquale has picked up Wiff Stamen and Fizz Nichols," Rocco said.

"With a small arsenal," Pasquale replied. "A little over an hour ago, a cruising unit was passing the Arriwani Hotel when the room clerk ran into the street yelling bloody murder. Your two friends were on the second floor, weapons in hand, kicking in doors. When we booked them, they kept yelling for you and Lyon."

"This is all tied in with the killing of Junior Haney, and I want to know how," Murdock said.

"Simple enough," Rocco replied. "Fizz was with Junior the first time he met a man known as Rainbow."

"Who paid for Llewyn's murder," Murdock said.

"Exactly."

Murdock shifted his weight and stamped out his cigar on the floor. Sergeant Pasquale glared at the smudge. "All right," Murdock said as he stood. "Let's discuss the matter with those little bastards."

Fizz Nichols bent double and crumpled to his knees when Sean Murdock's extended fingers jammed into his solar plexus. Pasquale grabbed Murdock's coat and spun him around.

"I'm telling you only once, Captain. Cut that shit out in this town. Understand?"

"I was just opening the conversation," Murdock said as he backed across the interrogation room and leaned against the wall.

Still gasping for breath, Fizz glared at the fat police captain. "Get him out of here. We'll talk to Wentworth, not pig face over there."

"Fizz, you're going to highly regret you said that," Murdock said softly.

"Knock it off," Pasquale said. "Murdock—out."

"They're from my town, Sergeant. I want to know the deal."

"I said out."

Murdock glared at the diminutive Hartford sergeant. "You'll regret that too, wop."

Pasquale took a step toward Murdock with raised fists. Rocco stepped between them, parried the blow, turned Pasquale around and propelled Murdock from the room. Pasquale shook himself as if to shake off obscene things and then turned toward Fizz and Wiff.

"Now, let's hear. Why in hell were you two breaking into hotel rooms with guns?"

"We were going to waste the son of a bitch."

"Who?"

"Rainbow," Wiff said. "Fizz figured out where the room was. He killed Junior with his colors on."

"Who killed who?"

"Rainbow killed Junior."

Pasquale turned to Rocco. "Obviously Rainbow wasn't there, or we'd have these guys on homicide."

"Look at these pictures," Rocco said as he handed Fizz several photographs they had taken from Bea's collection. "In this first one there are three men. Do any of them look like Rainbow?"

Fizz took the pictures and examined them carefully. He moved across the room to stand under a light and looked again.

"Well?" Pasquale asked.

"I'm not really sure. You know, I didn't get a hell of a good look at him. Maybe it's this guy in the center."

Lyon, Pat and Rocco moved quickly to peer over Fizz's shoulder.

"Good Christ!" Pasquale said. "That's the governor."

"Well, I knew he looked familiar," Fizz replied.

"Could it be either of the other two men?" Lyon asked, knowing that Ted Mackay was to the right of the governor.

"These guys have gray and white hair," Fizz replied. "I did see that Rainbow had sort of brown hair."

"It could have been dyed," Rocco pressed.

"Maybe. I just can't be sure."

"I'd put them in the high-risk category," Rocco said as they drove in the Murphysville cruiser from the Hartford police station to the Arriwani Hotel. "I don't know that I'd have posted their bond."

"I owe them something," Lyon replied.

"And I still owe you guys from last time," Pasquale said. "I'll try and get the charges reduced."

"I'd appreciate that."

The Arriwani Hotel was a long, narrow building stuffed between a new office building and an ancient theater that now showed X-rated movies. In its more affluent days it had probably housed vaudevillians playing the theater; now its clientele consisted of welfare recipients, pensioners, and gray-haired men and women wearing loose-fitting clothes and purposeless expressions. The room clerk had obviously been recruited from the last-named group.

The clerk's skin was pulled tight across his balding head, and his rheumy eyes looked at the entering men with a mixture of fear and distrust.

"Your name's Warren, right?" Pasquale asked.

"I thought you were all through with me, Sergeant."

"These men want to ask you some questions. I expect you to cooperate with them fully."

"Yes, sir."

"The room that was broken into—who was it rented to?" Rocco asked.

"There were two. A Mr. Jones rented them both and paid a month in advance."

"Come on, Warren," Pasquale snapped. "Jones? You can do better than that."

"No law says I have to ask for identification. Jones he said, Jones I wrote down. He paid in advance and had two suitcases."

"Why two rooms?" Lyon asked.

"Mr. Jones said he was expecting friends."

Rocco stepped closer to the desk and loomed over the clerk. Warren retreated until his back was against the mailbox slots. "I didn't do anything."

"Did Mr. Jones's friends arrive?"

"Arrived. Stayed a few days and left."

"Who were they?"

"I don't know, just a couple of bimbos. Jones rented the rooms. I never did get their last names. Real lookers; you'd hardly know they was hustling."

"First names?"

"Penny and Boots."

"Tell us about Jones."

"He came in about two weeks ago, rented the rooms and paid in advance, like I told you. He was hardly ever there; then, when the girls came, they had men friends. I figure he was pimpin' for them."

"Did you see who they . . . entertained?"

"No. Around here it don't pay to look too close."

"Describe Jones."

"About late thirties, medium build, wore so-so clothes—just a guy."

"Could you identify him again?"

"I don't know. He wore sunglasses, the kind that go far around and have mirrors in them."

"Look at these." Rocco spread the photographs on the desk. "Do any of these men look like Mr. Jones?"

"They all look older than Jones. I'm not sure."

"Do you know anything more about the girls who came to the second room?" Lyon asked.

"They was just bimbos, mister. Young, good-looking, they didn't—wait a minute, there is one thing. When they first checked in they was ordinary enough, but one night I was on the second floor and their door was open a crack and I could see in. The room was filled with stuffed toys. You know, teddy bears, dolls, stuff like that. And the two dames had on little girls' clothes. It was weird—they looked like they was twelve years old or something."

"Let's see the rooms."

The two rooms Jones or Rainbow had rented were on the second floor on the street side of the building. The wood on both doors had been shattered when Fizz and Wiff had kicked them in, and at Rocco's touch the doors yawned open.

Lyon leaned against the doorway as the two police officers began to go through the first room. With precision and little wasted motion, they unspokenly divided the rooms between them and began their search. The rooms themselves were nondescript, grime and must matching the colorless decor.

The first room had obviously been occupied by the women. Two hairpins were found on the floor, along with a lipstick, smudged pieces of tissue in the wastebasket, and a pair of panties in the otherwise empty bureau.

More visible traces of the man remained in the second room. An open suitcase was on the bed, partly packed. A razor and shaving cream were still in the small bathroom; a chair had been overturned in the center of the floor.

"Looks like he was in a hell of a hurry to leave," Pasquale said.

"Only one suitcase left," Lyon said. "The clerk said he checked in with two."

"Oh-oh, lookee here," Pasquale said as he took a picture off the wall separating the two rooms. With the picture removed, a one-way mirror was revealed in the wall. A window in the man's room, a mirror in the women's. Sawdust near the baseboard indicated that it had been recently installed.

"A little voyeurism while the girls turned tricks," Rocco said.

Lyon knelt on the floor under the mirror. "Ten to doughnuts it's more than that." He felt along the dusty floor molding a moment, then went into the women's room and did the same.

"What do you have?" Rocco asked.

"Freshly bored holes through the dividing wall."

"He wired the joint," Pasquale said.

Rocco rocked on his heels. "Extortion."

"Classic," Pat replied. "The hookers set up next door, he gets his mark up here for a good time, pictures and sound of the whole party."

"Who?" Lyon asked.

"Well, we've got a hell of a lead," Pasquale said. "Two hookers, Penny and Boots—we'll put a make on them. I've never heard of a hooker yet who hadn't been pulled in half a dozen times. We'll get the room clerk to go through the mug shots."

8

Warren chuckled as he turned the heavy pages of pictures. "These aren't mug shots. This is a gallery of the hotel's guest list."

"Quit the comedy and keep looking," Pasquale said and signaled to Rocco and Lyon to follow him back to his office. They sat in the small room holding paper cups containing some sort of machine-made instant coffee. It was hot, and little else.

"What about vice?" Rocco asked.

"Lots of it," Pasquale replied with a laugh. "No, seriously, we don't have a vice squad anymore. Gave up busting queers two years ago, and if we had to check out the massage parlors we'd need twice as many men. We handle the real weirdos as part of each section's general function."

"I thought the men on the beats might have come in contact with Penny or Boots."

"I put out the word at shift change a few minutes ago," Pat said. "No luck."

"Not surprising," Lyon said. "I don't think Warren will turn up anything either."

"Why's that?"

"This Rainbow, if he is involved in a little dirty-picture extortion, isn't about to use local talent for the job. Too risky."

"Imported stuff."

"I would think so," Lyon replied.

Warren knocked hesitatingly at the edge of the door. "I looked through the books you gave me, Sergeant. I know a lot of the girls, but didn't see Penny or Boots."

"But you would recognize them?"

"Oh, sure."

"All right, thank you very much for your time, and stay where we can find you."

"What about the rooms and the things in the room?" Lyon asked as Warren left.

"Negative," Pasquale replied. "Your Rainbow may have been in a hurry to leave, but not so much of a hurry that he didn't wipe the place clean. No usable prints, and the things he left were items that could be purchased at any discount store."

"I think we should try the photographs of Mackay on the room clerk and the motorcyclist again," Rocco said.

"It bombed out," Pasquale said. "Why bother?"

"Suppose we touch up the photographs, have an artist color the hair brown as they both describe it, even brush in sunglasses, we might get a possible."

"It's worth a try. We have somebody who can do it."

"I think we should find the local importer of talent," Lyon said.

"What?"

"There must be someone in town who is the local importer of ladies of the night."

"Christ, Lyon," Rocco said. "Ladies of the night? No one uses that anymore."

"Well? Who's our importer?"

"Big Nose," Pasquale said.

"Who?"

"Big Nose Carrelli."

The Grecian Urn Massage Parlor was quite attractive if you didn't look too closely and notice that the marble pillars of the reception room were papier mâché. It was located on the fifteenth floor of one of the newer office buildings, next to a stockbroker's office. As Lyon stepped into the reception area, he noticed two things: the young woman behind the desk, with the deodorant-commercial face, wore a transparent toga, and the music piped over the stereo system was a Bach fugue.

"May I help you, sir?"

"Well, yes."

"Name?"

"Lyon Wentworth."

"Only the first name." She laboriously printed L-I-O-N on the first line of a receipt pad. "Would you like the regular massage at twenty-five dollars or the de luxe executive massage at thirty-five?"

"I really didn't come for a massage."

"Have you ever been to a massage parlor before?"

"I once had a rubdown at the New York Athletic Club after a handball game."

"Are you for real?"

"I'd like an appointment with Mr. Carrelli."

She gave Lyon an oblique look, picked up a pink phone and pressed an intercom button. "There's a Mr. Wentworth here to see you, Mr. Carrelli." She listened for a moment and then replaced the receiver. "Straight through that door and second door on your left."

Lyon followed her directions, wondering over the difference between the regular and the executive massage.

Big Nose Carrelli was immersed in a sunken tub smoking an Egyptian cigarette in a chartreuse holder. His massive head with its large nose protruded from the colored bath bubbles that hid the bulk of his body.

"Close the door and sit down, Mr. Wentworth." He shifted his weight to get a better view of Lyon sitting on a straight chair. "Pasquale phoned and said you'd visit my establishment and asked me to give you my fullest cooperation."

"That's very considerate of you."

"Not really. He said that if I didn't, he'd bust the hell out of me and my place."

"He thought you could be helpful in locating some—some ladies for me."

"Do you like Proust, Mr. Wentworth?"

"No. In all honesty, even though I taught literature for a number of years, I have to confess I never finished *Remembrance of Things Past*."

"Of course. I don't believe anyone has except me, Mr. Proust, and the typesetter. Pity."

"I'm trying to locate two girls, Mr. Carelli. They're in their twenties, not from Connecticut, and are called Boots and Penny. One's a blonde and the other's a redhead, if that's any help."

"You understand, Mr. Wentworth, that in addition to running this establishment, I have occasion from time to time to act as an employment intermediary."

"So I've been informed."

"Recently there's an extensive market for cooperative young ladies, go-go dancers, exotics, masseuses. The demand is often hard to fill."

"I'm sure it is."

"However, at Sergeant Pasquale's urging, I will do my best to cooperate. Why do you want these particular young ladies?"

"Let's say that they have been highly recommended."

"We have many applicants, some with college education. I'm sure we can find two very satisfactory ladies."

"Not just anyone. I want Penny and Boots."

"Not uncommon appellations for my applicants. I'm not sure I can help you."

"These are specialists. They have a different thing, so to speak."

"That might narrow the possibilities. What is their area of entertainment?"

"Stuffed animals and little-girl dresses."

"Personally repugnant, but that does narrow the field. It is truly a time of specialization."

"We're not sure where they're from. It could be Boston, Providence or New York."

"Not New York. The ladies from Fun City seem to think that Hartford is the end of the world. Vegas they'll go to, Hartford never. Boston or Providence. I will make inquiries."

"I appreciate your aid, Mr. Carrelli."

"Any time. But you really should dip into

Swann's Way again. A gold mine, a veritable gold mine. I will call you."

Big Nose called him four hours later. "The items you are interested in can be found at the Penobscot Hotel in Providence."

"Thank you."

"My pleasure."

If the Arriwani Hotel in Hartford had been transported in its entirety to Providence, and had there been a bar on the first floor, Lyon would not have realized that he'd changed cities. The Penobscot Bar was entered from the hotel lobby through swinging leather doors.

Although it was only four thirty in the afternoon, Lyon's eyes had to adjust to the dim interior. The bartender's elbows were propped on the bar as he leaned over in conspiratorial conversation with a woman in the corner.

Lyon slid onto a backed stool and waited to be noticed. Finally the woman tapped the bartender on the arm, and he turned to scowl in Lyon's direction. He moved along the duckboards in a painful shuffle.

"Feet hurt?"

"You know it. Bunions. What'll you have?"

"Sherry. Dry Sack if you have it."

"No sherry. I got some red on ice. It's not bad if you drink it fast."

"That'll do. I'm looking for some girls."

The bartender poured wine and shrugged his head toward the woman at the end of the bar. "Want me to buy her a drink for you?"

"I do if she's Penny or Boots."

"They're not here."

Lyon shoved a ten into the bartender's shirt pocket. "They come highly recommended."

"Drink's on the house. I might be able to reach them." He shuffled painfully across the floor and dialed a phone hidden behind the Carstairs. After a whispered conversation he came back to Lyon.

"They'll be down."

The blonde sat on the stool next to Lyon and pressed her knees tightly against him.

"You must be Penny?"

"My fame precedes me. I'll have a scotch and water."

"Where's Boots?"

"On her way. Takes her ages to get dressed. We usually don't come out this early. You want a party?"

"I thought perhaps we could all have dinner together."

"Dinner?"

"You must eat sometime."

"What about the party? We do some interesting things."

"Party?"

"It's sixty for both of us. We show you a real good time."

"I just want to talk, to ask you a few questions."

"You some kind of weirdo?"

"I don't think so."

"Boots and I like to go together whenever we can. Sometimes we go solo, but we prefer it together. We do almost anything you want—no whips or that sort of thing."

"I wasn't really dwelling in that area."

She gulped her drink, and another appeared before her. Lyon slid a bill across the bar.

"You some kind of cop?"

"No. I want to ask you about your recent visit to Hartford."

Penny pushed her drink back across the bar and stood up. "Uh-huh. No deal. It's been nice talking with you."

She turned to go as Lyon grasped her arm. "Wait. A friend of mine in Hartford said you—you were terrific. He gave me a recommendation."

"Sixty for the two."

"All right," Lyon said as he slid off the stool and followed her into the lobby of the hotel, wondering if he had sixty left.

They lived on the sixth floor of the hotel. Boots, the redhead, dressed only in bikini panties and bra, stood before the bureau mirror working on her hair. She turned to smile as Lyon followed Penny into the room.

"Hi, sweetie. Good deal—now I won't have to get dressed the rest of the way. Or does he want the little-girl bit?"

"Don't stop on my account," Lyon said.

He looked around the room. It was fairly large for that kind of hotel. He was taken aback by the number of stuffed animals that covered the chair, the dresser and the bed. Teddy bears, pandas, stuffed ducks, cats and dogs. A stuffed Wobbly doll sat on the windowsill. Oh, Jesus, he thought, *The Whores and the Wobbly*. It would never work.

"Put the money on the dresser, hon," Penny said as she slipped out of her blouse.

Lyon found he had three twenties and three ones in his wallet, and hoped he had enough gas to get back to Murphysville. He put the money on the dresser and turned toward the two women, who were busily clearing stuffed animals off the double bed.

"Come on, baby, take it off," Penny said as she slipped out of her skirt.

"Want me to warm you up a little, hon?" Boots asked as she twined her arms around Lyon's neck.

Lyon smiled at her and ducked his head under her arms and sidestepped away. He noticed that she slipped the money from the dresser.

"You want to play or not, baby?" Penny asked.

"He's the shy type," Boots said.

"I want to talk about Hartford."

Boots turned vehemently toward Penny. "He's a goddamned cop!"

"He sure didn't look like one."

"I'm not," Lyon said. "I want to know who hired you for the Hartford trip, and whom you entertained."

"You're a fed. They use the clean-cut type."

"No. I promise you. I am no type of law-enforcement officer."

"All right, then," Boots said. "Take off your coat."

"I don't want to party. I want to know about your trip."

"Take off your jacket and we'll see if you're a cop."

Lyon slipped off his jacket and hung it over his arm.

"Okay," Boots said. "Now turn around."

As they both sat on the edge of the bed, Lyon turned around. "He's not wearing a gun."

"Exactly what do you want, mister?"

"It's extremely important to me to find out why you went to Hartford, and who sent you. I know you stayed at a place called the Arriwani Hotel, and that a man called Jones paid for the rooms and that you entertained someone."

"If you know so much, why ask us?"

"Who hired you and whom did you entertain?"

The two women looked at each other. Boots shrugged. "Information all you want?"

"That's all."

"Well, you paid your dough. But no party?"

"No party," Lyon replied. "Who hired you?"

"Never did know his real name. Called the bar one day and said he'd really fix us up if we came over to Hartford and did a job for him. Mailed us five hundred in advance."

"What did he look like?"

"Gee, I don't know, just a guy."

"He told us to take the bus over to Hartford and go to this hotel where he had a room rented," Penny said. "He wanted to take some pictures, and then we just had to party one guy."

Boots laughed. "We gave out a couple of freebees while we was there."

"Like housewives," Penny giggled.

"Who was the man you entertained?"

"We weren't supposed to know," Penny said.

"Mr. X," Boots added. "Mr. X turned out to be ready teddy."

"He was kinda weird in the sack."

"You never knew his name?"

"Rainbow gave us a thou when it was over. We figured for that kinda money it's better to not ask questions."

Lyon spread the photographs on the bed and gestured to the girls to examine them.

"Hey, this is him," Penny exclaimed as she picked up one of the photographs.

Boots took the picture. "That's him all right. I'd swear to it."

"How could we forget?"

Lyon sank onto the bed. He felt weak and yet exalted. It was over. Finally they had a positive ID on Rainbow. He smiled up at the girls. "And you'll positively identify this man as Rainbow?"

"Rainbow? I don't know about that," Penny said as she dropped the picture of Ted Mackay on the bed alongside Lyon. "But I sure in hell know this guy."

"We balled the hell out of him," Boots added. "But what a weirdo."

"Right. That's the guy we were paid to party."

9

"ALL RIGHT, WENTWORTH. WHERE IN HELL HAVE YOU BEEN?" Bea sat Indian-fashion on the double bed, her arms folded across her chest, the shortie nightgown far above her knees. Lyon stood in the doorway and smiled at his wife.

"You don't really want to know."

"What?"

"You don't want to know," Lyon said in a raised voice. He sat in the rocker by the window.

"HOW MUCH DID YOU SPEND?"

"I'm not quite sure. Bail for the two guys; then there was sixty to the prostitutes."

She reached for the small hearing aid on the night table and adjusted it in her ear. "You're right, I don't think I want to know. Rocco wants you to call as soon as you can."

Lyon moved tiredly to the phone and dialed Rocco's home number.

"Herbert here."

"I found the girls in Providence."

"I'll be right over."

"Can't it wait until morning?" Lyon found himself speaking into a dead phone.

"What girls?" Bea asked.

"You'll never believe—"

"Try me. It's *my* hide someone's after." As Lyon recounted the events, Bea had glasses perched on the edge of her nose and made notes on her clipboard. She looked up as he finished. "Well, outside of Ted Mackay's secret sexual predilections, which don't surprise me, we have four people who have seen Rainbow. The motorcyclist, the room clerk, and the girls; but none of them can give you a positive identification."

"Not yet, but we're getting closer. The question now is, what's the best way to proceed?"

"Talking with Mackay?"

"Exactly."

"Lyon?"

"Hmmm?"

"You didn't . . . I mean after the interview with those two women . . . Were they bad-looking?"

"Not bad for their type."

"What's their type?"

"No, they weren't bad. They had a Wobbly on the windowsill."

"Oh, God."

"Of course I didn't."

Again that day, a woman's arm twined around his neck.

When Bea and Lyon entered the study wearing matching terrycloth robes, they found Rocco Herbert in the leather chair with a drink.

"You want some ice for that?" Lyon asked.

"Better pour yourselves one."

"What's up?"

Rocco threw a folded newspaper across the room. The article was on the front page near the bottom, centered under the picture of a beauty-contest winner.

CYCLIST KILLED IN MISHAP

> Fitzsimmons ("Fizz") Nichols, 28, of 3 Bracecourt Lane, Breeland, was killed today when his motorcycle was forced off the shoulder of Route 29 by an unidentified vehicle. State police ask that any person or persons viewing the accident phone the Breeland Barracks.

Lyon dropped the paper, where it was retrieved by Bea. He walked to the window and looked out. Far below, the Connecticut River curved around the Seven Sisters promontory and began its path toward the sea.

"Well?" Rocco asked as he poured another drink.

Lyon slowly turned. "I think you had better call Pasquale in Hartford."

"Christ! The room clerk."

"It could have been an accident," Bea said.

As Rocco punched the number of the Hartford Police into the phone, Lyon crossed and sat next to Bea. "You don't really believe that?"

"No, but it's always possible."

"You said we had four people who had seen Rainbow; now there are three."

"No, there aren't," Rocco said as he hung up.

"What happened?"

"Warren was shot a little more than an hour ago. During an attempted robbery of the Arriwani Hotel. Once through the forehead with a forty-five."

"Any witnesses?"

"Nobody saw a thing."

"Can you get the hookers in Rhode Island pulled in?"

"There's a Lieutenant Troagland over there who went to the last Criminal Justice Seminar with me."

"For God's sake, Rocco, call him. Get those girls in custody. Room 641 of the Penobscot Hotel."

Lyon walked through the living room and out the French doors onto the patio above the river. He sat on the edge of the parapet and felt the breeze in his hair. He kicked off his slippers and felt the rock against his toes.

They passed before him in silent procession like dead characters at the end of a long-ago film. Junior with his last word; Fizz sleeping under the pool table; Warren looking through the mug shots with a lascivious grin; and Llewyn, bright and hopeful.

All leads pointed toward Mackay, but the girls said that someone had paid them to entertain Ted Mackay . . . was that Rainbow? Or could there be more than one? The pieces weren't making sense. The only certainty was that Rainbow, whoever he was, was methodically obliterating his trail by killing everyone who had any means of identifying him. As soon as they got close . . . Lyon sat up and hurried back to the study, where Bea had just finished telling Rocco about the Providence trip.

Rocco looked up. "Bea was telling me about Mackay and the girls. Jesus."

"We've got a leak, Rocco. We've got a leak a mile wide."

"Rainbow is covering himself. First Fizz, then Warren . . ." A look of shock came over the big man's face. "My God, he couldn't know our movements. Only a few of us knew."

"Sergeant Pasquale."

"Impossible. I've known him for years."

"Murdock?"

"Someone," Rocco said. "Someone."

Sarge's Bar and Grill had been opened several years before on the outskirts of Murphysville. Master Sergeant Renfroe, one-time company first under Captain Herbert, had come to visit his old company commander and had stayed. Large bottles of pig's knuckles molded along the bar, and Renfroe scowled if a customer asked for anything other than beer and a shot, although he did keep a bottle of passable sherry hidden under the bar for Lyon.

"The fuzz is here," Renfroe whispered as Rocco and Lyon entered.

"Damn it all, Sarge, I'm the fuzz," Rocco said.

"This is foreign fuzz, over in the corner booth."

Pat Pasquale sat morosely staring into a short beer.

"What's the matter, Pat?" Rocco asked as they slid into the booth.

"Why couldn't we have met somewhere else? This beer is flat."

"I thought it would be convenient for you. What's new on the Warren killing?"

"Nothing. Headquarters calls it a felony murder in the act of robbery."

"We know better, don't we, Pat?" Rocco asked with a bite to his voice.

"What does that mean?"

"Only us'ns and you knew about the tie-in between the room clerk, Rainbow and Fizz. Now, I'm sure about us, but not—"

Pasquale rose and leaned across the table. "You shut your goddamn mouth before you even suggest such a thing."

Rocco's hand went across to push the small officer back into his seat. "You listen. You know that Fizz Nichols was knocked off?"

"Pushed off the road. Happens all the time to those crazy cyclists."

"And Warren the same day?"

"Coincidence."

"Bullshit."

"I don't like your suggestion, Rocco. I don't like it one bit, so knock it off."

"Pat, are you involved in this?"

Pasquale's hands reached across the table and grasped Rocco's uniform collar. "Listen, you big son of a bitch, I'm not listening to this crap."

"Yes you are."

"Wait a minute," Lyon said softly. "There could be another answer. Someone else, say in Hartford headquarters, could have pieced things together, seen Pasquale's reports."

"Reports aren't finished yet. No one saw them."

"There must be another reasonable explanation."

"Wait a goddamn minute," Pasquale said. "Are you two playing Mutt and Jeff with me?"

"Yep." Rocco grinned.

"That's dirty. For God's sake, you've known me for years. The three of us worked on the Houston case together."

"Let me bring you up to date," Lyon said. He

recounted the previous day's trip to Rhode Island, telling Pasquale about the girls and their revelations, and his and Rocco's conviction that Rainbow was systematically exterminating possible witnesses.

"What about the hookers?" Pasquale asked.

"Rhode Island called me at six this morning. They have them in custody."

"Did the leak come from your office somehow, Pat?"

"Anything is possible, but I don't think anyone besides myself had all the pieces."

"That narrows it down, doesn't it?" Lyon said.

"Murdock," Pasquale replied.

"What do you two know about our Captain Murdock?" Lyon asked.

"We know him only by reputation," Rocco said. "He's the meanest bastard in the state. Hell of a rough guy, but runs a tight town. I think everyone's scared to death of him."

"ALL RIGHT, YOU GUYS, WHAT ARE YOU UP TO?"

They turned in unison to see Bea standing in the doorway.

"You want to use the phone, miss?" Sarge asked.

"Make me a pink lady," Bea answered and slid into the booth.

"Last time I was in New York, they even had women in McSorley's," Rocco said.

"And the Yale Club," Lyon added.

"I never even saw a pink lady," Sarge yelled across the room.

"Give her a beer," Lyon yelled back.

"You know, you guys, I'm the one they're after. I want in."

"You're under guard," Rocco said.

Bea looked across the room to where Jamie Martin was leaning against the bar. "He's a nice boy, Rocco, but this morning I went grocery shopping, and he insisted on carrying the bags."

"He used to be a bagger at the A&P before he joined the force."

"How's he going to draw his gun when he's carrying an armload of groceries?"

"To tell you the truth, I sometimes wonder if he still doesn't think that metal thing on his hip is for marking soup cans."

"Thanks," Bea said and grabbed the beer Sarge delivered.

"Let's get organized." Lyon said. "Pasquale, you go to Rhode Island, make a deal with those girls."

"That makes sense."

"Rocco, you're the one to beard Murdock. You know the approach. And before I talk to Mackay, I want to find out a lot more about our majority leader."

"Like what?" Bea asked.

"What sort of man is he? His law practice, his family, where is he vulnerable and why. I want a profile on the man. I've got a feeling he's our key to this whole thing."

"I'll do that," Bea said firmly.

Lyon put his hand on her arm. "No, hon, I'd rather. . ."

"Uh-huh, Lyon. This one is mine. Jamie can tag along."

"She can get more information than you can—and faster," Rocco said.

"Bat your pretty eyes, dear," Pasquale said.

"That's sexist, Sergeant," Bea said.

"Use your political clout," Rocco suggested.

"That's unethical."

"Come on, Bea, compromise: be a sexy state senator with clout; we need it."

"You seem to have given everyone his instructions; what about you, Lyon?"

"Me? Why, I'm going for a balloon ride."

10

The Farquith Inn was far enough from the city of Hartford to provide a sense of intimacy, yet close enough for those who could afford an extended lunch hour. Bea sat in the Antique Room, ordered a gimlet, and waited for Harry Schwartz. Harry was Ted Mackay's law partner in the firm of Schwartz and Mackay, and, because of Ted's political involvement, the working head of the firm.

He slid into the booth next to her, and she felt his knee press against hers. Harry Schwartz was debonair. His hair was styled, his clothes mod without clashing with his attorney image, and his eyes constantly flirted.

"Hello, darling," he said and kissed her. "What a delight to have lunch with you. I've been hoping for months."

"I'm glad you could come, Harry."

"I think you should know that I am completely dishonorable at lunch—dinner too, for that matter."

"I wanted to talk about Ted Mackay," Bea answered and looked across the room toward the bar, where Jamie Martin in plainclothes sipped a ginger ale.

"Spoilsport. Why does everyone want to talk about Ted when I'm the interesting one?"

"I know you are, Harry, but you're not the one I might campaign with next month."

"Such reserved for us who toil in the shadows."

"Honestly, I need your help."

"Anything I can do, Beatrice. You know that."

She felt his leg press firmly against hers. "There are some people who want to put Ted and me on the ticket, but we just don't seem to hit it off."

"Opposites eventually attract, dearest."

"Do you really believe that?"

"No."

"Tell me about Ted. I want to get to know him, to understand him. I've got to, Harry. I must establish some sort of relationship."

He leaned back in the booth as the soup was served. She sensed a subtle change in his manner, a partial dissipation of his facetiousness. "Theodore Rachman Mackay. What do you want to know?"

"Everything. It will all help."

"Bea, I can't tell you how much I want Ted to get the gubernatorial nomination and win the general election."

"I'd expect you to be a loyal supporter, Harry." To her chagrin, Bea found that she was doing all the things she'd said she wouldn't do. She had returned the pressure of his leg, left her hand under his, tilted her head in a coquettish manner, and kept her hearing aid on.

"You don't understand. I didn't say I was a supporter of Ted. I said I wanted him to get elected."

"Are we playing word games?"

"As Ted says, let me clarify my position. With Ted governor, our law partnership has to be dissolved, which is something I've been wanting to do for the past year and a half."

"I think I see a skeleton through a crack in the closet door."

"Not a full-fledged one; perhaps a few flecks of bone, but not a whole skeleton."

"What are we getting at, Harry?"

"Let me bracket the man for you. Ted grew up in the east side of Hartford, where the plaza is now."

"I remember the area from when I was young. The slums along the river were torn down for an urban renewal project."

"That's the place. He worked his way through Boston College working nights as a presser in a laundry. He came out of World War II a captain and thought he saw gold at the end of the tunnel, and that the best way to obtain the sheckels was to get a law degree. I've seen the old profit-and-loss statements on how he did when he practiced alone in those early years. The truth of the matter is, he averaged less than six thousand a year."

"I thought all lawyers were filthy rich."

He squeezed her hand. "Some of us are, dear, but the way they're turning them out of law school these days, we're all going back to six thousand a year. Anyway, he finally managed to get himself elected to the school board. This is where I come along, a bright young Jewish lawyer looking for a handsome goy beard to round out a firm. I saw a good thing in throwing in with Ted. He's good-looking, articulate, and has a foot in the political doorway. With Ted active in politics and my holding down the fort at the office, we'd have a good thing going, and we did—until Ted got too greedy."

"You're not trying to tell me that Ted's on the take?"

"Of course not. We're watched pretty closely in this state; you have to attain national office before you become so obvious. No, Ted began playing all the ends against his middle. Nothing overtly dishonest, no flagrant violations of the canons of ethics; a few well-placed calls to the Public Utilities Commission, suggestions that certain clients hire our firm if they had any expectation of favorable legislation. What I call gray lobbying."

"You went along with it."

For the first time Harry Schwartz averted his eyes and stared across the crowded dining room. When he continued, his voice was faraway and low. "That's right, I went along with it. And now I've got a son who dropped out of law school and lives in a commune up in the Canadian woods. Does that make any sense to you?"

"I think so."

"I found I didn't need all the money, Bea. For a long while, I thought I did, but Ted's gotten worse in the last year. I want out, a graceful out, and that's why I want him elected and why I will deny everything I've told you."

"We've all seen it happen. The edge of the ethical line is awfully narrow, and one day the big opportunity comes along, and it's easy to cross over."

"And I want our relationship severed before that

big score happens down the road." He smiled. "Now, as for you, dearest, your best bet is to get on that ticket with Ted as lieutenant governor, then maybe you'll luck up and become governor by default when they hang him. In the meanwhile, maybe I'll luck up this afternoon."

Harry suggested an after-the-meal drink at the motel down the road. Bea declined, pleading a massive headache.

The face of the woman who opened the door of the Dutch colonial was slightly out of focus. Ted Mackay's wife blinked in the bright sun and her eyes narrowed. "Is that you, Beatrice?"

"Hi, Wilma. I was in the neighborhood and thought I'd stop in."

"Oh, Ted's not here. He said he'd be late tonight."

"I want to see you, Wilma."

Wilma Mackay blinked, and then a hesitant smile began and quickly disappeared. She stepped aside and waved Bea inside. It was two in the afternoon, and yet Wilma had to hold to the edge of the sofa with both hands as she fought to keep her eyes aligned on Bea.

"How nice of you to stop in, Beatrice. I see you so seldom lately. Perhaps you'd like a drink? Not that I usually do in the afternoon, but this is a special occasion, isn't it?"

"Thank you, Wilma. Anything that's easy."

Wilma Mackay disappeared into the rear of the house and returned with two orange blossoms. She seemed more relaxed as she handed one to Bea and sank on the sofa.

The woman sitting before her exhibited a pattern that Bea had found becoming much too prevalent among the housewives of her acquaintance. It seemed to start as husbands became more successful, children grew, and the preparations for the evening cocktail hour started earlier and earlier, until finally the pretense was dropped and the vodka drinking began early in the day.

They chatted amiably, Bea taking the part of the slightly younger woman asking advice of the older. Children—Wilma's were now in college and seldom home. The house—how difficult to keep help these days (Bea cringed). They had another drink, and Wilma's face dissolved even further, the facial lines seeping apart, the eyes squinting to keep Bea in focus.

"That's a nasty bruise you've got on your arm," Bea said.

Wilma tried to pull her puffed sleeve down over the black welt on her upper arm. "I—I fell. . . . I—Ted did it. He's so angry these last months, and my skin bruises so easily, sometimes he even—" She stopped quickly, realizing even in her present state that she had said too much.

Bea understood that there wasn't a great deal more she could find out. Ted's wife had established that recently he had exhibited a proclivity for violence, and his law partner had indicated that ambition and monetary success had become intertwined and an integral part of the man's personality. Everything she had learned pointed to the fact that Mackay was capable of instigating everything that had happened.

"I don't get out very much. My balance, you know. I have trouble with my inner ear," Wilma said as she drained half the glass.

"Yes, so I've heard. It will be difficult for you if Ted is nominated and elected governor, all those functions. . . ."

"Ted and I have already talked about it. His sister will act as hostess. I'm not up to it."

"That's very considerate of him," Bea said.

She didn't stay long; it wasn't necessary. As she was leaving, Wilma offered her another drink and, when Bea declined, made herself another.

Sergeant First Class Buck Kincaid had fought in two wars as a personnel clerk, but had doctored his own records to award himself a Purple Heart and two Bronze Stars. The assignment to the Army reserve unit was his last, and in three years he would retire.

Bea stood in the armory doorway and watched the sergeant's eyes as they slowly surveyed her body. She realized she was standing with the light to her back, which would clearly outline her figure through the thin summer dress, and she stepped quickly into the office.

"Nice, but you like them heavier," she said.

"Well, yeah," he said with a slow smile.

I'm not about to play that damn game again today, she thought to herself. "I'm Senator Wentworth," she snapped, and slapped her card down on the desk before Kincaid. "From the State Investigating Committee." If he didn't inquire into that too closely, she was in good shape.

He snapped to attention, his face turning to that compliant but stern look career enlisted men cultivate. "Yes, ma'am. What can I do for you?"

"The committee is investigating conflict of interest between members of the legislature and the federal government. Since some of our representatives are active reserve officers, I wish to see their files. You have them here?"

"Yes, ma'am. We have a duplicate of everything the Department of the Army has except for the efficiency reports."

"I'll start with Senator Mackay's. I believe he's a reserve colonel."

"Yes, ma'am. He's commander of the unit."

The 201 file was bulky, with the current material toward the front and everything dated. She found what she wanted near the rear of the file: a personal letter of commendation from General William "Wild Bill" Donovan of the OSS to First Lieutenant Theodore Mackay for his activities during the period March 1 to August 4, 1943.

She put the papers back into the file, slipped the letter of commendation into her purse and gave the file back.

She sensed the sergeant's eyes on her back and legs as she left the office. She couldn't help smiling a little.

For the third time, Captain Sean Murdock's foot pounded into the naked man's groin. The man clutched himself with both hands, groaned, turned his head, and lay in his own vomit.

"Read the rest of the arresting report," Murdock said to the uniformed sergeant seated at the desk in the interrogation room.

"Substances later identified as controlled drugs were found on subject's person."

"Not drugs?" Murdock asked with wide eyes and false incredulousness.

"Yes, sir," the sergeant replied.

"You don't mean you were going to sell drugs to the impressionable youth of Breeland?" the captain asked the prone man.

There was a groan from the floor in reply.

"My, my," Murdock said and kicked the man in the teeth.

"Subject resisted arrest and was subdued by

Officers Miller, Hattigan and myself," the sergeant continued in a monotone.

"Injured as a consequence," Murdock said, and kicked the man again with his steel-tipped shoe.

"You're going to kill him," Rocco Herbert said softly from the corner of the room.

"No I'm not," Murdock replied. "The bastard already has bail posted. But I'll tell you something. I seriously doubt that he'll peddle his junk in Breeland again. Will you, buster?" His foot crunched on the man's fingertips, and Rocco heard a bone snap.

Rocco was nauseated. He had heard of Murdock's tactics over the years but had not realized half an hour ago when he sat in the captain's office that he'd be a witness to them.

"In most places you bust them and they're out on bail by dinnertime, having cocktails at some fancy restaurant. Here in Breeland we make sure they aren't ready for any fancy meals for a long time."

"What about lawsuits?" Rocco asked.

"You got to have the prosecuting attorney in your pocket and full cooperation from the force."

"You really find it works?"

"Hell, yes. Come on, I'll show you. We've got a candidate in the fridge right now."

It had started out as a routine interrogation, with Rocco observing. Then the captain had forced the suspect to undress for a search, and then the first kick.

"He's passed out, Captain," the sergeant said.

"Dress him and throw him out. Come on, Rocco, I'll buy you a drink."

The City Hall Bar and Grill was across the street, and it took two drinks before Murdock began to talk about his dogs. His Great Dane bitch had just whelped, and the event was the source of a seemingly endless number of anecdotes.

"Cutest damn things you ever saw. Long damn legs, can hardly stand up. Hot damn, I love those dogs!"

Rocco signaled for another drink. "You know, I'm interested in your technique, Sean. I've been having trouble over in Murphysville with the kids. No respect; they just don't seem to give a damn."

"Lean on them and they'll learn. Hell, man. You're a big son of a bitch, you'll have everybody in town scared shitless of you in no time."

"Okay," Rocco said. "So you stomp the creeps, but I have a more serious problem. Can't convict, and leaning on the bastard isn't enough. Isn't nearly enough."

Murdock twirled the ice in his highball and looked into the glass. "Use your imagination," he finally said.

"Hell, I can't do it. I'm too conspicuous, and everyone knows me in town. And I can't trust the men on my force to do it. I thought maybe you had some contacts."

Murdock shrugged. "Some departments have a cooperative attitude."

"Like how somebody wiped out Fizz Nichols?"

"Not us."

"You know it wasn't an accident."

"Didn't say it was. You want somebody to call about your little problem in Murphysville?"

"Appreciate it." They drank silently for a while.

"If we help you out, we expect a little tit for tat."

"I understand. Who do you suppose got to Fizz?"

"Who knows? Something's up. The police commissioner calls me the other day and says any info I have on Rainbow or the killing of Junior Haney, I was to pass on to Ted Mackay."

"That's political. No way for me to get involved."

"Don't blame you," Murdock said and signaled for another drink.

Lyon caught the phone before the completion of the first ring. Bea, Rocco or Pasquale should be reporting in—perhaps Bea first. "Bea?" he asked.

"Robin Thornburton, Mr. Wentworth. I'm Stacey's daughter."

"I remember you, Robin, although it's been a long time. I understand you've given up a promising career as an infantry platoon leader to become a sculptor?"

"That's the problem, Mr. Wentworth. As soon as I told my father I was turning down the Academy appointment, he's had me jogging every morning and firing rifles every afternoon. It's interfering with my work, and his, too."

"He's a fine artist."

"I know he is. I tell him that he's one of the best children's illustrators working today."

"What does he say?"

"That when World War III starts they'll give him a star."

"I wonder if there'll be enough time to pin it on."

"I don't know what to do. He's sending the outline of your book back."

"Has he had any bourbon?"

"Booze?"

"Exactly."

"No. He's been on a diet for the past couple of weeks and hasn't had a drop."

"I'm sending down a case tomorrow. When it arrives, find something to celebrate."

"I'll try, Mr. Wentworth. As soon as it gets here we'll celebrate, even if it's the conquest of Carthage."

Lyon stared down at the incomplete manuscript of the children's book on the desk before him. He had to complete it, for his and Bea's sake, for Stacey's sake, and yet recent events seemed to obscure thought and prevent further progress. He put his head on his arms over the typewriter and tried to think.

"COME ON, WENTWORTH! We're out busting our backs and you're taking a nappy-wap."

Lyon looked up to see Bea and Rocco standing in the door. "I was thinking."

"You were sleeping."

He went into the kitchen and felt the percolator and found it still warm. He poured a cup of coffee, yelled over his shoulder. "Report, troops."

"Pat called from Rhode Island," Rocco yelled into the kitchen. "He's made a deal with the girls, and when we need them they'll cooperate. If they do, Pat and Rhode Island drop all charges against them."

"Great."

"In addition, Captain Murdock tells me that Ted Mackay used clout to have police installations report all information concerning our investigation."

"Then Mackay knew all about our trace to the hotel, Warren and Fizz?"

"It would seem so. Murdock's also involved in a little excessive police work, and claims that there's a group of senior police officers throughout the state who are acting as vigilantes. Something similar to certain South American countries and their death squads."

"Is there any tie-in?"

"There could be. It's not much of a step from roughing up criminals to the decision to rectify the political system."

Lyon looked thoughtful. "Up to now everything's pointed to Mackay. This is a new angle."

"Mackay might have wanted to know about the progress of the investigation out of curiosity."

"That's some curiosity."

"I've got something," Bea said. "I looked up Mackay's Army record. During World War II he was in the OSS, served overseas, and made a parachute jump into occupied France to operate a clandestine radio."

"Where does that lead?"

"His cover name during the operation was—"

"Rainbow," Lyon said.

They stood in the living room like the couple in the Grant Wood painting, although in this instance the husband held a silver cocktail shaker and the wife's eyes were out of focus.

"Get the hell out of here!" Ted Mackay yelled at Rocco and Lyon.

Wilma Mackay turned to her husband with a furtive gesture and plucked at his sleeve. "I thought you'd want to see them."

"You thought wrong. Chief, you have no authority in this city. And as for you, Lyon, are you some sort of police nut who likes to drag along after Herbert?"

"I'm perfectly willing to get a warrant," Rocco replied. "I think I have enough for several counts."

"Counts of what? Jaywalking?" There was a sanctimonious assurance in Mackay's stance.

"Perhaps everyone would like a drink," Wilma said with a birdlike flutter.

"Get one for yourself," Mackay snapped at his wife. "And make sure you take a couple of quick shots while you're out in the kitchen."

"Oh, Ted, I really don't—"

"Go on!"

Rocco waited while Wilma made her way from the room with the careful and methodical steps of the alcoholic.

"Sit down and shut up." Rocco's tone was quiet, and perhaps that made it even more sinister.

As Ted Mackay sank back in a chair, his eyes flicked across Rocco's determined face. "You can't talk to me like that." His tone, for the first time, was unsure.

"Yes, I can. Now listen and answer." Rocco's voice was still at a low register. "A young man named Junior Haney was stabbed to death in a bar. You had met Junior."

"I meet hundreds if not thousands of people. I'm a politician."

"We back-tracked Junior and the man who hired him to a hotel in Hartford, and from there to two girls from Providence. Those girls have identified you, Mackay. They know who you are and will so testify."

Mackay exposed them to his famous smile. "So, I played a game with a couple of harlots. I can give you a list half a mile long of those who have done the same."

"Then the room clerk was killed."

"This has nothing to do with me."

"Yes, it does. There is no one in this state who stood to benefit more from the death of Llewyn and the attempted murder of Bea Wentworth. You had a motive, Mackay—the gubernatorial nomination."

"This is nonsense."

Rocco crossed the room to tower over the cringing state senator. "You knew about the room clerk and about Fizz Nichols trailing Rainbow. You're one of the few people who did know, because Captain Murdock told you."

"I was interested in the case."

"I'll bet you were. You've heard the name Rainbow before."

"Yes."

"You're Rainbow."

"No, you've got it all wrong."

"It all points to you."

"No, it's wrong. I couldn't be. I'm not. I can prove it. Rainbow is going to call me tomorrow."

11

"Tell them about the pictures." Wilma Mackay's voice slurred as she held tightly to the doorjamb. "The ones with you and those two . . . "

"Don't, Wilma."

"I wasn't supposed to see them, you know," she said to no one in particular. "They just arrived in a plain brown envelope, like those things do. But that day curiosity got the better of me."

"After half a fifth, no doubt," Ted said harshly.

"I think you had better tell us exactly what's been happening," Lyon said.

"Do that, Ted. But I don't think I want to hear it." Wilma turned from the room and disappeared down the hall.

"I don't have any choice, do I?"

"Not unless you'd rather we booked you," Rocco replied.

Ted Mackay seemed to dissolve before them. The strong, photogenic features slackened, the jaw line relaxed, and his shoulders sagged as waves of inchoate anxiety and weakness surfaced to control him.

"I think I'd like a drink. You two?"

They shook their heads as Ted left the room and went down the hall.

Lyon's gaze fixed on the empty doorway, and he spoke without turning to face Rocco. "I'd go after him if I were you. You'll probably find him in the study down the hall.

Rocco hurried through the door. A short scuffle could be heard from the far reaches of the house. Rocco returned, pulling Mackay by the arm, and flung him across the room toward the couch.

The .25- caliber automatic dangled loosely from Rocco's hand. He forced the slide back to eject the live round in the chamber, extracted the clip and put the weapon into his pocket. "He was in the study. The gun was in his hand." He turned toward Mackay, who had slumped on the couch. "It's not going to be that way, Senator. However, if you tell us all you know, we can help you."

Mackay looked up with red-rimmed eyes. "She drinks too much; she never used to do that. Sometimes I hit her, and I never used to do that."

"What happened after the pictures arrived?" Lyon asked softly.

"He called me two days later—that was the day of Llewyn's murder. He said they'd taken care of Randy Llewyn for me. I told him he was crazy, and he laughed at me and told me I didn't have any choice. It was done, and if I didn't cooperate, the pictures would be sent to dozens of people around the state, and the tape recordings—he played part of one over the phone. They made me sick."

"And you cooperated with him?"

"Yes, I had to; you see that, don't you? He told me that the way would be open for me to get the nomination, that what I'd have to do for them would be minimal."

"Them?"

"I don't know. He acts like there's a whole bunch of them. A whole band of fanatics."

"Your contact was always with the same man?"

"Yes, by phone. I got the call at the law office. He wouldn't identify himself to the receptionist, and at first I wasn't going to talk, but in politics you never know, so I took the call. 'This is Rainbow,' was the first thing he said. That was my Army code name years ago. I didn't know anyone even knew about it, but he seems to know everything there is to know about me. At first he didn't ask for much—a little information here, a little there. Items I'd give out to almost anyone. Then he became insistent about information regarding the investigation of the Llewyn killing. For that, he sent me money—five thousand dollars. A token, he said, and there'd be more, he said."

"The buy was complete." Lyon recalled how in the recruitment of espionage agents the passing of money was considered a necessity to ensure the reliability of the recruited. Maybe only a few dollars for expenses, but money had to pass to ensure the compromised position of the man bought.

"And if you get the nomination and win the election, they'll want other things from you," Rocco said.

"Of course, but I had nowhere to turn. There's no way out for me. They have me."

"You must know who Rainbow is," Lyon said.

"No. I don't. I never saw him, only talked by phone."

"He was able to take pictures and tape-record you and the two women. How could he have known that you were with them at that particular time?"

"I was set up. Like a drunken salesman from Albuquerque, I was had. An envelope marked personal and confidential arrived at the office; inside was a scrawled note that said a couple of friends of Heddy's would be in town soon and would I be interested. It gave a time and place. There were pictures of the two girls dressed in those silly dresses and holding stuffed animals. There were also some pictures where they didn't have on a stitch."

"Who's Heddy?"

"Sometimes when I go to New York on business I stop in to see Heddy. She lives on East Eighty-ninth Street."

Rocco looked thoughtful. "And Heddy dresses up for games also?"

"Yes."

"He must have followed you, found out Heddy's brand of entertainment and decided to use the information. What about the postmark on the envelope, the note—where are they?"

"I destroyed them. I couldn't leave pictures like that around. I have young women working at my office," Ted said indignantly.

"When is he supposed to call you next?"

"Tomorrow, first thing in the morning."

Lyon looked at Rocco, and the chief nodded. "I'll stay with him, but I think we had better bring Pasquale into it."

"Not Murdock."

"You know it."

At eight in the morning, Wilma Mackay's hands shook as she served coffee to the men assembled in her living room. She had forgotten the cream, and Lyon noticed that when she returned from the kitchen her hands had steadied, and he suspected that another bottle of vodka had been opened.

Ted Mackay, his assurance dissipated, sat on the couch and looked at the living-room phone as if it were an obscene object. Pat Pasquale, earphones around his neck, sat before a recording device and phone amplifier. Rocco stirred his coffee incessantly.

"How long for a trace, Pasquale?" Rocco asked.

"Two minutes, if you can keep him on that long. I have the state police on standby. It's a long shot, but you never can tell."

"That allows for a lot of leaks," Lyon said.

"I haven't told the units the nature of the case. There's no telling how deep infiltration goes."

The phone rang at five past eight. Mackay looked bewildered.

"Pick it up, damn it," Rocco said in a guttural whisper.

Mackay reached tentatively for the phone and gingerly lifted the receiver. The recording device and amplifier were switched on so that others in the room could hear the conversation.

"Hello," Mackay said in a weak voice. "Is that you, Rainbow?"

"Who the hell do you think it is?"

Mackay looked at Lyon, and Lyon nodded. "I've got problems with Wentworth."

"What about him?"

"He's traced everything to me. The girls, the

information leaks. He wants to make a deal, Rainbow."

"What sort of deal?"

"He wants ten thousand dollars. He says if he gets the money today, he lays off and brings his wife around. I need her backing, Rainbow. I've got to have it or the convention goes into a deadlock."

"Ten thousand is not impossible. Can we trust his deal?"

"Yes, I'm sure of it."

There was a long pause on the phone. "All right, you and Wentworth be at Rambler's restaurant at eight tonight."

"I know the place."

"You'll get further instructions there. And remember, Mackay. I know you, you don't know me. Any cops, any undercover men, and a long list of people get your pretty pictures."

"I understand."

At the sound of the dial tone, Pasquale was immediately connected to a phone company supervisor. He talked in a low voice for a moment and then hung up. "Sorry. There just wasn't enough time."

"It looks like Ted and I have an appointment at Rambler's," Lyon said.

They pulled Mackay's Chrysler into the crowded parking lot and sat a moment before entering the restaurant. An odd place for the first contact, Lyon thought. Rambler's was well known in the area as a Hartford political hangout. The state chairman, always one or two city council members, and a few members of the legislature would be crowded around the small bar or eating in the main dining room.

"You'll be well known here," Lyon said.

Mackay followed Lyon inside. They had taken all possible precautions. A signal device attached to the chassis of Mackay's car would give out a constant tone that Rocco and Pat could follow. In addition, Lyon had a small transmitter in his jacket pocket.

Rocco and Pasquale would be out of sight nearby.

Inside the restaurant the decor was mostly in reds. Chandeliers sparkled and seemed to sway to the loud conversation coming from the bar.

"Good evening, Senator Mackay." The maître d' bowed and ushered them to a table. A waiter instantly appeared.

"The usual for me and sherry for Mr. Wentworth."

"Why would he choose this place?" Lyon asked.

Mackay pointed to a phone jack on the floor. "He's making it convenient for us."

The drinks were served and they sat silently before them. The conversation of the other diners swirled around them. Several men came to the table to pass a word with Mackay, but he quickly excused himself with an "I'll get back to you."

It was half an hour before the phone was brought to the table. Mackay looked at the red instrument before him and picked up the receiver.

"Hello. . . yes . . . he's here with me . . . no, no one else." He listened intently for a moment, then fumbled in his breast pocket for pad and pencil. "Let me write it down," he said as he scribbled notes. Then he hung up.

"Well?"

"He gave me instructions for the next call."

Lyon slid behind the wheel as Mackay looked at the notes he had taken.

"Where now?" Lyon asked.

"Down Farmington Avenue and left on Haynes."

"That's one way. We'll be going the wrong way."

"He said to follow instructions exactly, that he'd be watching."

Lyon threw the car into gear and they lurched forward. He felt his palms dampening and tried to drive carefully. Cars passed; traffic lights seemed to have malevolent eyes as they blinked red on their approach. He felt impatient, and sensed the dejection in the destroyed man sitting next to him.

Traffic lights eventually turned green, and they proceeded to Haynes Street, where they made the wrong-way turn and continued to the next thoroughfare.

"Next!" Lyon had to yell before Mackay responded.

"Go across the bridge and continue on the highway to Exit Ninety-seven. Make a left and drive into the supermarket parking lot. Drive at exactly forty miles an hour."

Rainbow's plan was simple and safe. Wrong ways and a slow rate of speed made the spot on any tails easy. Rocco and Pasquale would have to lag far behind and depend on the electronic device to give them a proper tangent. Lyon had the utmost confidence in the large and small police officers and knew they would be careful to avoid suspicion.

They turned off the highway and into the empty supermarket parking lot. The great expanse of asphalt was broken by an occasional street light, and long shadows crossed over the lot. Lyon slowed the car to a stop near the solitary phone booth at the end of the complex. He glanced around as they waited and knew why Rainbow had chosen the spot. On either side and to the rear of the shopping center were broad expanses of fallow Connecticut Valley tobacco fields. The desolate rows gave a field of vision on this clear night of hundreds of yards in either direction. If Rainbow was watching, any car near the one that Lyon and Ted occupied could be easily seen.

The phone rang.

Mackay sat unmoving as it rang again. Lyon reached across the car seat, opened the far door and shoved Mackay. He stumbled, grasped the edge of the car door, and staggered toward the phone booth.

He talked for a few moments before returning to the car. "Rainbow says we leave the car here. There's another car parked in back of the buildings with the keys in it."

It was a nondescript Chevy. The engine turned over on the first try and hummed in a low, even monotone.

"We're to go back to town," Mackay said. "Repeat the instructions he initially gave us exactly in reverse."

"Where are we going?"

"The cathedral. He says he and his people are monitoring police and CB bands, so don't try and get the word to anyone, or the whole deal is off."

Lyon felt the light weight of the small transmitter in his jacket pocket. He calculated the odds and decided to follow Rainbow's instructions.

The cathedral loomed stark and white against the clear night. It was a massive building constructed of hewn blocks of Vermont marble, with a steeple that cast a long shadow across the low steps leading to the interior.

As instructed, they parked the car in the rear lot against the building, hiding its shape in the shadows of the towering edifice.

"You go alone," Mackay said huskily and slumped into his seat.

Lyon entered the building from an unlocked side door. The door opened directly into the nave near the altar. Candles burning before the side-altar railings, and low lights in the high ceiling, cast a dim illumination through the interior.

He stopped by a pillar at the edge of the long lines of pews and glanced down at Mackay's note pad in his palm. "Fifteenth pew from the front, right-hand side. Folded newspaper with further instructions."

He counted back and walked the line of pews past the folded kneeling rails. The newspaper was midway up the line. He sat down and pulled the paper toward him. The center fold opened, and a typewritten message slid to the polished seat.

THIRD CONFESSIONAL FROM THE FRONT DOOR.

The confessionals were on the far side of the church toward the main entrance. He entered the third one and sat on the hard bench.

"You wish absolution, my son?" The sonorous voice issued from the darkness behind the latticework.

"Rainbow?"

He was answered by a low laugh. "What's the deal, Wentworth?"

"I lay off you and Mackay and bring my wife around."

"For ten thousand dollars?"

"Exactly."

There was a pause from behind the latticework,

and Lyon shifted uncomfortably. "Rainbow, you there?"

"Right here, Wentworth."

He felt the barrel of a pistol pressed against the back of his neck. "I thought we had a deal?"

"We do." A package wrapped in brown paper was thrust into Lyon's lap. "It's all there in fifties and hundreds; count it when you get home. Don't move for ten minutes after I've gone," the muffled voice said.

"I understand." He pressed his elbow against the small radio in his side pocket. He couldn't reach for it yet. Any move and he'd be killed.

"I want a public announcement of your wife's switch in support by noon tomorrow. See that it hits the noon news. If I don't hear it, those men guarding your wife will be no match for us. We'll kill her, do you understand?"

"Yes."

"Remember, ten minutes. Don't move. *Les jeux sont fait*."

Lyon remained in the confessional without moving and thought he heard footsteps retreating rapidly across the church. He breathed deeply and let his hand slip into his pocket to extract the radio. He thumbed the transmission switch.

"Rocco. Rocco, can you hear me?"

He turned the set to receive and heard only static. The thick stone walls and the heavy steel girders crisscrossing the ceiling overhead were creating an impenetrable barrier for either transmission or reception on the small radio.

Lyon ran for the door.

They sat in the study at Nutmeg Hill and stared morosely at the money spread across the card table.

Bea shook her head. "And he got away."

"It was a good attempt," Rocco said.

"And Lyon could have been killed by that madman."

"It was easier for him to buy me off."

"Well, I'm not bought off," Bea said. "I'M NOT BOUGHT OFF AT ALL. I'm announcing publicly tomorrow, all right. I'm announcing for Mattaloni, and you can do what in hell you want with that money."

Lyon picked up a handful of bills from the stack on the table. "I'm going to do something with the money, and I'm going to do it first thing in the morning."

12

The next morning at Murphysville Police Headquarters it took them less than an hour to trace a good many of the hundred-dollar bills. The newer ones, a good portion of the lot, had come from the Fifth Federal Reserve District in Boston. An unctuous money vault clerk, after telephoning back to assure himself that they were indeed calling from police headquarters, had assured them that the newer money had been recently delivered to the Nutmeg National Bank.

"God almighty," Rocco said. "That's the biggest bank in the state."

"It's all we have," Lyon said comtemplatively.

"The bills could have been circulated anywhere in the state."

"We've got a listing of twelve bills in near sequence. I think they came out of Nutmeg in a lot."

The chief tilted back his chair and sighed.

The main office of the Nutmeg National Bank was in a new building near the Hartford Civic Center. As Rocco and Lyon entered the lobby from Main Street, doors hissed open almost silently as they stepped onto the thick pile carpeting. The Main Street level of the bank was a branch banking floor, with the executive offices in the upper stories. As he walked past a counter, Lyon picked up a folded financial statement and flipped it open as they stepped into the elevator.

A quick scan of the foldout sheet informed him that the Nutmeg National Bank had assets in excess of one billion dollars, 102 branches throughout the state, and over 137,000 depositors. He underlined the last figure and leaned toward Rocco.

"We're reducing the odds."

"Christ, Lyon. You're the only man I know who thinks 137,000 to one is good odds."

The doors of the self-service elevator opened when it leveled at the fourteenth floor. They stepped into a reception area where a petite blonde with a scrubbed face sat before a litter-free desk.

"May I help you?" she asked.

"We have an appointment with Lehigh Collins," Rocco answered.

A nearly surreptitious phone call by the receptionist, a ten-minute wait on uncomfortable modernistic chairs, and they were finally escorted down a long hall to a large office and an annoyed Lehigh Collins, vice president.

Collins stood behind his desk and offered a quick

handclasp. "Chief Herbert, Lyon. Sit down. I'm sorry I don't have much time, I have a loan committee meeting in a few minutes."

Lyon handed Collins a list of the money serial numbers.

"We need your help in tracing some money," Rocco said.

Collins tapped his fingers on the folded sheet without scanning the numbers. "That's not my department, Chief." He reached for his phone. "Security does a good deal of that funny money stuff for the federal people. I'll be glad to refer you."

"We'd rather keep it in the family for the time being," Lyon said.

"I don't understand."

"Yesterday, ten thousand or more of that money was withdrawn from this bank. We want to know who drew it out."

"I'm in real estate investments, Lyon. You know I'd like to help out a neighbor, but I'm just not equipped—"

"We would like the request to come from you, without mention of police interest," Rocco said. "We'd prefer that others in the bank were kept in the dark about the origin of the request."

"Chief Herbert, you know how I appreciate all you've done for Murphysville. In fact, I said that at the last town meeting. Those talks you gave to the third grade on bike safety were excellent. I really can't help you, but I will refer—"

"Collins." Rocco's voice took on the hard but underplayed edge that Lyon had come to recognize. "I was up to your place last week. That fence around the new swimming pool is only three feet high."

"That fence cost damn near as much as the pool."

"Town ordinance says four feet. I guess I'll have to drive up to your place after we leave here."

Collins glared at Rocco, tapped the list again, took his glasses from his breast pocket, and then smiled. "Extortion, Chief. Out-and-out extortion. What do you want to know?"

"The Federal Reserve says that some of those bills were recently shipped to your bank. They were probably drawn out at the same time, hundreds and fifties—an unusual request, I would think, ten thousand in cash."

"Not so unusual as to arouse undue interest. We do have depositors who go to Vegas, or perhaps even gamble in town; some just like to keep large amounts of cash around for strange reasons. Some businesses still pay in cash. Some large corporations maintain thousands in petty cash."

"In hundreds?" Lyon asked.

"Well, that's true," Collins said reflectively.

"The thing is," Rocco asked, "can you trace it?"

Collins thought for a moment. "Not exactly. What I mean is, I'm not sure we can pinpoint cash to an individual account."

Lyon leaned forward. "You're on computer?"

"Of course."

"You can run a few days for any account that withdrew ten thousand dollars or more."

"We're the biggest bank in the state. We have hundreds of corporate accounts."

"I'm not interested in corporations. Tax regulations, new rules on political contributions, auditors; I don't believe the money would have come from a corporate account. I think it came from an individual's account."

"That would narrow it quite a bit."

"Then you could run your records to find if such a withdrawal was made—in cash."

"We could run the teller slips first, then match those against individual accounts—yes, it could be done."

"It has to be done soon. I can't tell you how important it is," Lyon said.

"It would have to be at the end of business, sometime tomorrow when I could get free time on the computer."

"Will you get the list to me as soon as you can?"

Collins shook his head sadly. "If I don't, I don't think I could ever drive home without getting a summons."

Rocco gave a low laugh. "That might be true."

As they rode down on the elevator, Rocco turned to Lyon with a puzzled look. "Where in hell did you learn about banking functions and computers?"

Lyon was thinking about a large elephant caught in an elevator, and the pathos for children it might engender, and he didn't answer.

The rally for Mike Mattaloni was being held in the Breeland High gymnasium. Lyon stood under the basketball scoreboard and leaned against the wall as two men waving chicken drumsticks from the box dinner walked past. Bea was in the center of the gym floor gesturing with a chicken wing at the prospective candidate and other supporters. He looked at the soggy box in his hand and wondered why he always got the backs at these functions.

Rocco Herbert, looking uncomfortable in an ill-fitting suit, crossed the floor toward him.

"I'm hungry as hell," Rocco said. "All I got were backs."

"Impossible. I got all the backs. Stop in the house after we leave and I'll feed you a couple of steaks."

"You're on." The police chief stood next to Lyon against the wall and looked appraisingly around the gym. Jamie Martin, also dressed in mufti, was next to Bea, while another Murphysville officer was by the main door. Captain Murdock stood by the punch bowl scowling, as if he disapproved of the whole affair.

"What about Murdock?" Lyon asked Rocco.

"I don't know. I've had some talks with my brother-in-law on the state police, but we don't have anything conclusive. Murdock's enforcers, or whatever they are, are well insulated underground."

"If it's not him, it could be anyone else in this room."

"Or outside. How in hell can I protect Bea?"

"I don't think he'll try anything without assurance that he can get away."

"In other words, a calculating nut."

"Exactly."

"All right, then it won't be in the building, but we have a hell of a problem when we leave. It must be a good fifty yards to the parking lot. There's a rise to the right, and the football grandstands to the left; anyone with a high-powered rifle—"

"There's only one floodlight outside the building."

"I guess so. I didn't notice."

"Knock out the light. It's my feeling that if he plans to do it, he plans to get away with it. He'd have to be a good distance away, and he'd need the illumination of that light."

"It's the start of the convention tomorrow. It has to be tonight."

"Take out that light, will you, Rocco?"

The chief nodded and slipped out the door. A

Breeland officer walked over to Lyon. "You Mr. Wentworth?"

"Yes."

"There's a phone call for you on the pay phone in the hall."

He knew who it would be. It was the same distant and muffled voice.

"I heard the news on radio and television, Wentworth. What in hell's going on?" Rainbow said.

Lyon gripped the phone tightly. He knew what he had to say, and he didn't want to say it. "She won't back down."

"You took money." The enraged voice was strangled.

"I said she won't back down. She says it's a matter of principle. I'll give you the money back; just leave us alone."

"You bastard. She's a dead woman, Wentworth. She's dead."

The dial tone hummed in Lyon's ear, and he hung up with a cold chill.

Rocco was coming down the polished hall. "I had to break into the fuse box, but it's done."

"Our friend just called."

"Threats?"

"To say the least."

Rocco looked off into the distance. Lyon had seen that look years before in Korea when the Ranger captain had been ordered to capture an insignificant hill in order that some obscure point could be made at the peace table.

"All right," Rocco said. "Let's get her out of here. Martin rides with you. Keep Bea down in the back seat. I'll follow in my car, and we'll get more men out to the house. Well, don't just stand there. Get going!"

"THIS IS A NEW PANTS SUIT AND I AM NOT GETTING ON THE DIRTY FLOOR BOARDS."

Lyon turned from the driver's seat, put his hand firmly on Bea's head and pushed her below the level of the windows. "Come on now, cooperate."

"I don't like it one bit."

They had negotiated the distance from the school entrance to the now darkened parking lot at a half run, with a crouched Rocco shielding Bea, while Lyon and Jamie Martin flanked either side. Rocco gestured from the Murphysville car as it pulled alongside the small Datsun. Lyon started the car as Jamie eased his police special from his holster.

"I think this whole thing is a lousy idea," Bea's muffled voice said from the back.

"He's going to make a mistake, Bea. Somehow and somewhere he's going to blow it, and we'll have him. We're already beginning to bracket him. We know a lot more about Rainbow than he realizes."

"Like how he's going to kill me."

"And more."

"Like what?"

"That he's from this state and lives within twenty or so miles of here. He has to be; he reacts too quickly."

"He lives here like two million others."

"He's male, Caucasian, thirtyish, near six feet with a medium build."

"That narrows it to half a million."

"Slight Boston nuance to his voice, a certain inflection even though his voice has been muffled. He seems to know us."

"One of my constituents. That lowers it to one in a hundred and fifty thousand."

Lyon tried to laugh. "Well, that's some progress,

and don't forget the French phrase he used on me, *les jeux sont fait*."

"That's the name of a book by Sartre. Translated, it means the bets are made."

"What did you say?" Lyon's foot left the accelerator, and he turned toward the back seat.

"I said Sartre."

"No, the translation."

"The bets are made, something like that."

"That's very interesting," Lyon said. He turned back to devote his full attention to the road and the onrushing night. Glancing in the rear-view mirror, he saw Rocco in the police car directly behind them.

He was filled with doubts. He should never have gotten involved. Even though attempts had been made on Bea's life, he should not expose her to further danger.

When they were first married they had gone backpacking on a portion of the Appalachian Trail. A montage of views of his wife on the trail ahead of him: turning with a toss of her head, a laugh, urging him on.

He saw her standing over the grave of their child, her eyes wide and dry, the tears used up as she turned toward him with bent shoulders.

"All right, Wentworth," heard a thousand times, and he loved her very much.

It was all drawing to a close. He had no doubt whatsoever that Rainbow would make a move—tonight, for it had to be before the convention.

Lyon concentrated on the probabilities and possibilities, trying to put himself in the place of their antagonist.

He must know that there was a heavy guard around the Wentworth house. Any type of frontal assault, even if successful, would be costly without the absolute certainty of success. Bea would be guarded in the morning, and the convention hall would be swarming with security. Granted, anyone can murder anyone at almost any time, but only on the basic assumption that the assassin will himself be captured or killed.

Another car could pull alongside and fire a weapon through the window, but there would be scant chance of hitting Bea. And it must also be obvious that they were being escorted by a police car.

He knew when and how it would happen. He turned to Jamie at his side. "What time is it?"

"Nine twenty."

"And we left the gym when?"

"I looked at the clock on the wall as we left—exactly nine ten."

Lyon knew it was a thirty-minute ride from Breeland to Murphysville, which meant they were within minutes of being halfway there.

He swerved the car onto the shoulder of the road. Jamie fell against the door as Bea sat up in the rear seat.

"Out!"

He jackknifed out and wrenched open the rear door. Grabbing Bea by the arm, he dragged her from the car. Jamie Martin was out his side with the pistol held before him as he crouched.

"What's happening?"

"Run," Lyon yelled. "Run!"

Grasping Bea's hand, he pulled her off the shoulder of the road. They stumbled into an adjoining drainage ditch and up a small bank. A wall made of loose stones ran the length of a field, and they clambered over it and lay in the high meadow grass.

"What is it?" Jamie asked again.

"Get your head down."

Brakes screeched as Rocco's car stopped behind the Datsun. A door slammed; heavy footsteps sounded as the two other officers stumbled over the wall.

"Down!" Lyon yelled at Rocco.

The chief looked at him for a brief instant and then threw himself prone beside them.

Orange flame illuminated the night sky as the Datsun blew up.

"Thermite, I'd say," Lyon said over the roar of the burning car.

"What's going on?" Rocco asked as he peered over the stone wall with the Magnum in his hand.

"He's made his second mistake, and we have a perfect setup," Lyon replied.

"Mistake? He came within twenty seconds of blowing you up."

"I'm curious," Lyon said. "Did he have it detonated on a time device, or was it engine heat?"

13

The state political convention had historically been held in the Haskell Auditorium immediately across from the state capitol. It was a large, pseudo-Grecian building, utilized for concerts, road-company plays, and other large meetings or performances.

State police ringed the building.

Kim eased the VW camper into a restricted parking area near the main entrance of the building. A state trooper with knife-crease pants and a hat that seemed to sit on the very top of his head walked briskly over to the camper.

"Move it, miss. Can't park here."

"Check with Captain Norbert," Kim replied with a smile.

The trooper looked at her doubtfully and then reached for the radio at his belt. He talked into the set for a moment and then looked back at the camper.

"Captain says it's all right." He gave a two-finger salute and walked away.

Kim turned to part the curtain that partitioned the camper and looked into the dim interior. Curtains pulled across the rear and side windows hid the occupants from outside view. Lyon sat at the small table making notes on a yellow legal pad, while Bea, across the aisle, looked toward him with her head slightly cocked. Rocco was stretched uncomfortably along the rear seat looking glumly over his folded arms.

"We're here, people," Kim said.

"You know," Rocco said, "eventually we're going to have to level with the news media 'bout the car bombing."

"How did it come out on the news?" Lyon asked without looking up.

"Like we gave it to them. Two unidentified bodies, male and female, were found in burned wreckage. They announced it on the seven and nine A.M. news, and the paper carried it on the front page. They'll be all over us for an ID of bodies that don't exist."

"Another couple of hours, Rocco."

Bea knocked on the table. "DAMN IT ALL, WENTWORTH, DO YOU KNOW WHO RAINBOW IS?"

Lyon held a finger to his lips. "Shh, dear. Yes, I think I do."

"Then for God's sake tell us."

"I could be wrong. All I have so far is conjecture and probabilities."

Rocco sighed. "Not enough for an arrest?"

"Not yet. But I think that before the morning is over, we'll have enough to take him."

"Since you seem to be running the Murphysville, Hartford, and state police this morning," Rocco said, "how about giving us our instructions?"

Lyon looked at the scrawls across the yellow pad. "All right, let's run through it. Registration is almost complete. In a few minutes I'll be going in. Do you have the field glasses and radio?"

Rocco handed him a pair of binoculars and a police walkie-talkie. "You're tuned in on the security band. Don't change the setting."

"Good. Is Jamie ready for the run to Providence?"

"He should be across the street in one of our cruisers right now."

Lyon made a check on his list. "When Collins comes with the list, will you see that the information gets to me?"

"Yes."

Lyon turned to Bea expectantly.

"I'm all set," she said. "No one except the chairman knows I'm here. He'll recognize me at exactly eleven forty-five to place Mattaloni's name in nomination."

"And I take her in through the stage entrance and directly to the podium," Rocco said.

"Security on stage?"

"We're using the podium built for the President's last visit. Bulletproof glass surrounds the speaker."

"Excellent."

There was a sharp rap on the camper's sliding door, and they gave a start as Rocco instinctively reached toward his holster. Lyon slid the door open a few inches and peered out. Satisfied, he opened the door further as Captain Norbert of the state police stepped inside and slid it shut.

"Will you tell me what's going on?" he asked Rocco.

"Protection for Senator Wentworth, Norbie. Told you that on the phone."

"Then why the big secret?"

"I'll fill you in later. How's security?"

"I've got fifty troopers here; we've surrounded the building and have men posted inside. Nine hundred and eighty people are in the building as of ten minutes ago. That includes delegates, guests, news and media people. No one can get in or out without being checked and issued a registration badge."

"They seem to go in and out all the time."

"All the men have radios, and if a call is put out to watch for someone coming out. . ."

"You can grab him."

"Thanks, Norbie," Rocco said. "I'll see you in a couple of minutes."

Captain Norbert shook his head and slipped out the sliding door. "No one tells me anything," they heard him mutter as he walked away from the VW.

"It's time for me to go in," Lyon said. Rocco nodded. "You know where I'll be."

There was another sharp rap on the door.

"You know," Bea said, "for a secret meeting, this is like Grand Central."

Sergeant Pat Pasquale stuck his head in and handed Rocco a seating diagram of the auditorium. "Clear in the lobby if you want to go in now."

Lyon leaned over and kissed Bea. "It's almost over now."

Lyon and Rocco left Pasquale with Bea and entered the main lobby, which was almost empty except for several troopers, a manned credentials desk and a photographer.

Every delegate, journalist or guest had to pass the credentials desk, present identification, be verified; then he was whisked to the small photography unit in the far corner of the lobby. The photographer took an instant picture while his assistant typed a card, affixed the photograph to the card and ran it through the laminating machine. The final result was the delegate's registration card for the two-day length of the convention.

His name checked off as a journalist by the credentials clerk, Lyon was directed toward the photographer. He stood where directed, and his picture was taken twice in rapid succession.

The clerk looked up. "What periodical do you represent, Mr. Wentworth?"

"The *Weekly Reader*," Lyon replied.

As his identification badge was being laminated, Lyon turned back to the photographer. "You have the duplicate pictures for us?"

"Right here, Mr. Wentworth, like you asked." The photographer handed Lyon a bulky envelope.

"And this includes everyone in the building?"

"Everyone with a badge, which is everyone except the police officers."

"There're nine hundred and eighty pics there," Rocco said.

"Remove all the ones of women, blacks, and individuals over sixty or under twenty. I imagine there will be fewer than three hundred left."

"And you think one will be Rainbow?"

"Yes, I do. How long will it take for Jamie to get to Providence with them?"

"Less than two hours, say another hour for the hookers to put a make on the photo, and then we'll have it." Rocco hurried from the building with the envelope of pictures.

Lyon left the lobby by a side door that took him up a flight of stairs to the second floor. He walked briskly past various offices and down a long, narrow corridor that ran along the side of the auditorium and ended at a small door. The door opened onto a small platform suspended above the floor of the auditorium to the far left of the proscenium arch. In addition to the spotlights mounted on the frame of the tower, it was occupied by a TV cameraman and a technician with earphones. The camera panned across the noisy assemblage on the floor of the convention.

The technician pushed the earphones down over his neck and glared at Lyon. "You authorized up here?"

"*Weekly Reader*," Lyon replied, pointing to his badge.

The technician clamped the earphones back over his head.

The heavy suspended lights would create a glare that would make those on the tower vague shadows to those below. Lyon sat cross-legged near the wall, spread the seating diagram across his knees, and began to scan the auditorium with the field glasses.

The state nominating convention was a microcosm of the national convention. Cities and towns, identified by signs, were caucusing on the floor, while messengers ran from group to group rallying support. The drone of voices filling the hall attested to the intensity of the fight over the nomination of state candidates.

The tail end of a demonstration left the auditorium by a side door, the kilted bagpipers attempting, with one last skirl, to make an impression over the din.

"What's next?" Lyon yelled to the cameraman over the tumult.

"Gubernatorial nominations."

"Good." He scanned the audience again, looking for familiar faces.

It would be an open convention. The incumbent governor had decided to retire, and that, combined with the death of Llewyn, left a political void. Support, so many local pundits explained, was evenly divided between Mackay and Mattaloni, with a large block of uncommitted delegates. Bea's placing Mattaloni's name in nomination was her outward show of support and was bound to switch many of the undecided.

Lyon felt a hand on his shoulder and turned to face a police officer.

"You Wentworth?"

"Yes."

"They asked me to give you this, said it was from a Mr. Collins at the bank."

Lyon took the neatly folded paper and thanked the officer, who disappeared behind the small door. He unfolded the sheet and ran his finger down the list of names. He was astonished at the number of people who, for one reason or another, saw fit to draw ten thousand dollars in cash from their accounts. He realized that he'd been looking sadly at the list of bank withdrawals for a long time. It was now almost complete; everything was falling into place. The din in the auditorium seeped into his consciousness, and he looked down at the audience.

"Who did they just nominate?" he asked the cameraman.

"Jeez, pay attention, will you? Ted Mackay."

Lyon looked briefly at the seating chart and then

trained the field glasses on row DD off center. He focused on the three men sitting near the aisle. Wilkie Dawkins, in his wheelchair at the end of the row, had a bemused look on his face and was making notes on a folded piece of paper. Danny Nemo, Wilkie's employee and perennial companion, leaned over and whispered something in the crippled man's ear. Both men laughed. Immediately next to Nemo, Ted Mackay sat slumped in his seat with his hands tented across his nose.

Lyon swiveled the glasses slowly over the auditorium and focused on the far wall, where a man stood near the exit doorway midway up the room. Captain Murdock, his arms folded across his chest, leaned against the wall. The last of the demonstration began to fade away as the chairman rapped for order.

The introduction of the next nominator began. As always, the name would be announced last, and the speaker would leave the wings and go to the podium.

The palms of his hands were damp. He realized that the source of his anxiety was not so much that they might be nearing the end of their search as it was fear over Bea's safety. If he was wrong, if his hypothesis was incorrect, her appearance on the podium would place her in grave jeopardy. He had to suppress the thought, and he trained the field glasses back on the audience.

". . . Senator Beatrice Wentworth." The chairman's rising voice was amplified through the hall.

Danny Nemo's hands grasped the edge of the seat in front of him as he slowly and incredulously rose to his feet. His face was colorless as he looked at Bea on the stage. He brushed past Ted Mackay, who looked up at him quizzically, and stepped into the aisle.

Wilkie Dawkins wheeled his chair to block his exit and grasped the edge of Nemo's jacket. Danny shook his head and tried to tear away as Wilkie's hands took a firmer grip. He shook his head vehemently, slipped out of his jacket, and gave the wheelchair a shove that sent it careening down the aisle, where it hit the side of a row and turned over to sprawl Wilkie across the floor.

Danny Nemo began to run up the center aisle as Lyon thumbed on the radio. "It's Danny Nemo. Do you read me?"

"I've got it," Rocco immediately answered. "Danny Nemo."

"He's going up the main aisle; Dawkins is near row DD."

"We'll get them."

As Rocco Herbert stepped through the double doors at the end of the center aisle, Danny saw him and turned back. Tandems of state troopers stepped through side doors and began to converge on the running man.

Drained of emotion, Lyon let the radio fall as Bea's voice echoed through the chamber. "I place in nomination the next governor of this state, Mike Mattaloni."

The building became a pandemonium of shouting delegates as a band swirled through the side doors at a trot, playing fast ragtime as they attempted to circle the room. Onrushing state troopers were caught in the middle of the demonstrators.

Rocco had reached Wilkie Dawkins and righted the chair and was attempting to push it back up the aisle.

Danny Nemo leaped to the stage and disappeared around the edge of the curtain as a trooper clambered after him.

They would have him in a minute, Lyon thought, and then it would be over. The women in Rhode Island would identify the picture, a bank teller would remember Danny's withdrawing cash from Dawkins's account, and it would be over. He glanced down at the list of names on the bank withdrawal sheet, where he had underlined that of Wilkie Dawkins.

It all fitted, there would be enough for an indictment. He fumbled for the radio and thumbed the transmitter button. "Rocco, do you hear me?"

"I'm in the treasurer's office with Dawkins, but we have a problem."

"He's raising all kinds of hell."

"That too, but the problem is Nemo. We can't find him, but he can't get out of the building."

14

Captain Norbert and Rocco Herbert were arguing outside the auditorium beside the VW camper. It was apparent that they were valiantly attempting to keep their voices subdued, but words carried, and nearby state troopers turned diplomatically away.

Lyon walked toward the two intense police officers. The strong feelings he had experienced on the camera tower had drained him; the temporary elation over the ending of the affair had been replaced by a deep lethargy. He walked between the two men, slid open the camper door, and sat down.

"I'm telling you for the last time," Norbert said. "No one, but no one, got out of that building."

"Damn it all, Norbert, take a look for yourself. People are coming and going all the time."

"Right, and they have to go past my men at the two open doors, badges are checked, photos are compared to bearers, and no Danny Nemo left the building."

Rocco looked over the state police officer's shoulder at the main entrance of the building. Small groups of twos and threes passed in and out of the building while officers, clip-boards in hand, examined everyone.

"And everyone has a badge," Norbert said.

"Then he's got to be in there still," Rocco replied.

"That's what I've been telling you. We're searching the inside now. If he's slipped back into the main auditorium, it will take longer, but he can't get out."

"I saw him go over the stage and around the curtains," Lyon said.

Captain Norbert glared at Lyon, obviously piqued at civilian intrusion. "Thank you, Mr. Wentworth."

"I know what he looks like; I'll slip in and circulate," Rocco said.

"Waste of time."

Both police officers turned in puppetlike unison to look at Lyon. "What?"

"I said it's a waste of time; he's not in there."

"How are you so goddamn sure?" Norbert asked.

Lyon stood to lean against the side of the VW. He was feeling better and wondered if there was coffee inside the building.

"Well?"

"Rainbow has been two steps in front of us the whole time. I doubt very much he'd make the grave tactical error of staying in the building."

"There's no way for him to get out without going past my men. Even without a make on him, his name is on his badge, and they've been instructed to detain anyone without a badge, or anyone with the wrong badge."

"Your men are the only ones in the building who don't wear badges." He began to walk toward the steps. "I'm afraid we're not going to like what we find."

Captain Norbert caught up to Lyon as he reached the first step, grabbed his arm and swung him around. "What's that supposed to mean?"

"It means you should cinch your search into small places in the building, places just large enough to hold a dead man."

"Who's dead?"

"One of your men. And I'd take a count of the cruisers."

Rocco looked stunned. "He's killed a trooper," He said in a low voice. "Killed him and taken his uniform."

"I would expect so," Lyon said. "We should have foreseen it. I'd have the men look in air ducts, cabinets—places like that."

Captain Norbert frowned at Lyon a moment, then signaled to a corporal holding a radio. He began giving commands.

It took fifteen minutes to locate the body, stuffed up a pipe shaft in the basement boiler room. The trooper was dressed only in underwear. His neck had been broken.

Captain Norbert turned away from the body, making guttural sounds in the back of his throat. "That bastard, that rotten son of a bitch. He won't get far."

"Not in a police cruiser, he won't," Rocco said, after word came that one was missing.

In the treasurer's office Pat Pasquale sat on the edge of a desk, while Wilkie Dawkins angrily rolled his wheelchair back and forth.

"I need to be back on the floor of the convention—do you understand that? Do you read me?"

"You're not going back, Dawkins," Rocco said from the doorway. "I'm charging you with accessory to murder, conspiracy to murder and attempted murder two counts. Pasquale's got you on the same for murder and extortion. It's a long list of charges."

"You are out of your mind! How could I murder anyone?" He pounded the arms of the chair with both fists. "Can't you see, damn it all? I'm a cripple. I can't even walk."

"Accessory and conspiracy to murder don't require pulling the trigger."

Wilkie tried to rise from his chair. "I didn't kill anyone."

"Danny Nemo did."

"I don't even know about that. Danny is only my employee."

"Exactly," Lyon added.

"I think there are some federal charges around somewhere," Rocco said. "Violation of civil rights."

"You big bastard!" Dawkins ran his chair forward with muscular thrusts of his powerful shoulders. Rocco sidestepped, and the chair smashed into the wall.

Rocco gripped Wilkie's shoulders with both hands. "Let me tell you something, mister. There's a dead trooper in the cellar of this building. I'll lay you ten thousand to one we'll find Nemo in a trooper's uniform. He was in a little bit of a hurry this time."

Wilkie fought for composure, backed his chair, and slowly took a cigar from his vest pocket. "What do you have on Danny?"

"Two witnesses identify him as the extortionist of Ted Mackay, and a trail back from that to a dead motorcyclist and to hiring the murderer of Llewyn."

Dawkins carefully lit his cigar and blew a smoke ring. "And how is that supposed to tie into me?"

"Money drawn from your bank account by a draft signed by you. Money we have traced back to you," Lyon said.

Wilkie sat back and silently comtemplated them for a moment. "And just why would I do that?"

"Power. You've controlled Ted Mackay for quite some time through financing his campaigns. But you knew Ted, and you knew that the ties weren't strong enough, and that with all your money you couldn't buy Ted the nomination with Llewyn and Bea in the way. You ordered them killed and had Ted told about it. He could vacillate—he might turn on Rainbow—so you insured the operation by the extortion pictures and the payoff money.

"With Llewyn and Bea out of the way, Ted might be elected; and you would control him two ways, your money and his fear of Rainbow. When we began to move closer to Rainbow, he killed Junior Haney, Fizz, and the room clerk to cover himself."

"This is ridiculous," Dawkins said. "This Rainbow must be a member of some nut group. Everything else is only your conjecture—all the evidence is tied to Danny."

"You don't think Danny is going to hang alone? He'll be caught, Wilkie, I promise you that. And when he is, he'll implicate you, just as we can implicate you through the money."

As they watched, a flicker of emotion crossed Dawkins's face as he rapidly weighed possibilities. He crushed his cigar out in an ashtray. "Gentlemen, please. You're building a whole massive conspiracy around me. And it's just not true. I was the financier—that and only that. I gave my money away. Oh, you'll go further back in the bank records, I'm sure of that, and you'll find other large cash withdrawals."

"In what total amount?" Lyon asked.

"Around a hundred and twenty thousand," Dawkins responded. "Now, I do admit that the money was given to a political organization. And it is true that you might fault me for backing an extremist group, but it was my money, taxes were paid on it, and the money was given in good faith for the ideals they stand for."

"You're a real patriot," Rocco said.

"I like to think so," Wilkie responded. "If this group involved itself in extremist activities such as political murder, then I had poor judgment. But I assure you I had no direct connection with those radicals."

"Only with Rainbow?"

"Rainbow being Danny Nemo, yes. But it was my impression that Danny was only a courier between me and the group. I had no idea he was actually involved in the things you tell me."

"What did you expect this group to do with a hundred thousand dollars?"

"Any organization is an expensive thing to operate. Money for literature, a staff, all sorts of expenses."

"And you have an accounting of those things?"

"Not yet, but I would expect one eventually."

"And the ideology?"

"It's not a question of ideology; it's a matter of power. With power all is possible, and ideologies can be formed to meet the need of the moment. It's really quite immaterial to me whether we go right or left. I'll take a stance when the time is appropriate."

"Where is this group located?" Rocco snapped.

Wilkie laughed. "Let us say that we are extensively organized throughout New England. And this is only the beginning."

"Then the group will be disturbed when they find you under arrest?"

"I don't really think it will come to that, Mr. Wentworth. But to answer directly, yes. I expect there will be massive demonstrations, pressure upon the media, the cry of frame."

The door opened and Captain Norbert stuck his head in the room. "Mackay's withdrawn; it's Mattaloni on the second ballot."

Dawkins rose in the wheelchair, his arms supporting his weight. "No! That's not the strategy, that's not what I told him."

"I think all this has been a little much even for Ted," Lyon said.

"I won't allow it!" Dawkins's face was flushed as he sank back in the chair.

Lyon wondered whether the man was mad, naïve, Machiavellian or just evil. Perhaps madness encompassed all of it. "It's over, Dawkins."

"A setback, a temporary setback. It's happened to all who sweep for power."

Lyon leaned forward to look into the opaque eyes of the man in the wheelchair. "There isn't any group, Wilkie. There is not now, nor has there ever been. You have a conspiracy that is not a conspiracy.

Danny Nemo was your general, soldier and nemesis."

"Danny was my gofer, my legs, a messenger. The group may have used him as an instrument, but that's all."

"All your contacts with this group were by letter or phone?"

"Of course. Individual cells, no contact, the secret of political success."

"And did anyone ever phone when Danny was present in the room?"

"Well, no. But that's coincidental."

"Is it going to be coincidental when we obtain a court order and locate his safe-deposit box?"

"What's that supposed to mean?"

"When we open Danny's safe-deposit box we're going to find close to a hundred thousand dollars of your money. Your seed money for a group that doesn't exist."

"Wait a minute," Rocco said. "You're telling us that all of this was a scheme to bilk Dawkins?"

"Yes. The inversion of a relationship. Danny Nemo preyed on the weakness that he knew so well. It was only meant to be two killings, Bea and Llewyn. The rest would be fire bombs, messages, threats . . . until the other killings became a necessity to cover the identity of Rainbow."

"Then there isn't any group?"

"There never has been. It was all Danny's creation exclusively for Wilkie."

Wilkie's eyes met Lyon's. "I hardly think I was so naïve as to have been duped through all this, Wentworth. It's not possible that I hired a male companion to act as my legs and he conned me, flimflammed me, created a whole edifice of which nothing exists."

"It's immaterial to me what you believe, Wilkie. I know there isn't any group, and that Danny Nemo acted alone."

Wilkie swiveled the wheelchair and rolled across the room toward the window. Rocco took a step toward him, but Lyon waved him back.

"There isn't any evidence of a political group," Wilkie said softly.

"None," Lyon replied.

"Which means that we're terribly clever or that I've been a fool." As he looked out the window, his hands gripped the arms of the chair, and when he spoke again his voice was far away. "After I was hit in Vietnam, I lay in a hospital bed for sixteen months; it gave me a lot of time to think, to plan on how not to be powerless ever again."

"Why don't you book him, Pat?" Rocco asked.

Sergeant Pasquale pushed off the edge of the desk. "Gladly."

The wheelchair spun in a semicircle until Wilkie faced them with a contorted face. "My group is here! They're all around us. They have to be. You won't get me from this building. Do you understand? I control the convention, this state; and they won't desert me!"

They watched the wheelchair leave the room as Pasquale pushed it into the hall.

"I'm not letting you out of my sight until we catch Nemo," Rocco said as they drove back to Murphysville. "Norbert will keep a tight guard around Beatrice."

They drove in silence until the radio began to sputter. Rocco answered the Murphysville dispatcher. "This is control, M-One. Captain Norbert says the car has been recovered and they suspect a ten-o-eight."

"Ten four." Rocco said and replaced the transmitter.

"What does that mean?"

"It means that Danny has dumped the police car and has probably stolen another car. I don't see how he'll get through, wearing a trooper's uniform."

"We found the dead trooper's clothes gone, but Danny's clothes weren't in the auditorium."

"He took them with him. He'll change."

"Exactly."

"Well, we'll cover the banks Monday morning. When he tries to get to his safe-deposit box we'll grab him."

"Perhaps," Lyon replied thoughtfully. "Perhaps."

"What do you mean?"

"I'll tell you later."

When they arrived at Nutmeg Hill another cruiser was in the drive, and an officer with a shotgun was stationed near the entrance to the house.

"Will you please explain . . ." Rocco tried to say as Lyon strode toward the barn. "Where are you going?"

"How many men are out here?"

"Half the Murphysville force—six guys."

"Good, we can get the Wobbly II in the air that much faster."

"The Wobb . . . your damn balloon? You're out of your living mind!"

Lyon entered the barn and trundled the hot-air balloon bag into the yard, and then returned for the remainder of the equipment. "Get your men over here. I'll tell them what to do for the launch."

"You'd be a sitting duck up there. It's hardly time for fun and games, and I'll be damned if my men will be a part of it."

Lyon grunted as he pulled the balloon bag from

the cart and began to spread it over the ground. "He's not around here—yet. The faster I can get airborne, the faster I can come down, and the safer I'll be. If you don't help, I'll do it myself."

Rocco watched Lyon as he intently aligned the bag in position. He shrugged and signalled to the remainder of the officers around the house. "Next you'll be selling snake oil," he said.

With the puzzled officers following the directions given them by Lyon, who was using a double blower to help force hot air from the burner into the envelope, the balloon began to rise over Nutmeg Hill.

Lyon leveled off at six hundred feet and made the proper adjustments to the propane burner. He looked over the edge of the gondola at the terrain surrounding his house.

The view was excellent and completely unobstructed. He was directly above the widow's walk, and by turning in either direction he had a panoramic view of the hills, trees and river.

North of the house the land ran flat toward the edge of the promontory, where it dropped off sharply to the river. A difficult approach requiring a boat to the rocks below, and a very steep cliff to climb up to the plateau on which the house sat. He discounted that possibility.

Due south was the drive leading down to the road. There would be traffic and a guard on the road—too dangerous. To the west, the stand of pines surrounded by heavy brush was uninterrupted for nearly a mile.

It would be from the east. Off Route 29 to the old quarry road, park down the hill a quarter of a mile from the house, then through the sparse woods to the barn and then the house beyond.

Yes, it would be like that.

He pulled the ripping panel. As hot air was released from the exposed side of the envelope, the balloon began a rapid descent. When he was twenty feet from touchdown, he called down to the waiting Rocco.

"From the east, Rocco. From the east."

"What in hell are you talking about?"

"Danny Nemo. He'll come from the east between eight and nine tonight."

"Will you get down here and tell me what you're talking about?"

Since Lyon didn't really think he was going to get any work done, he opened a new bottle of Dry Sack and poured a neat vodka for Rocco.

"It's going to occur to Danny," Lyon said after the first sip, "that it will occur to me sometime today or tomorrow that he won't go far without getting to his safe-deposit box, that there is a safe-deposit box."

"You've already thought about it," Rocco replied.

"That's something he doesn't know, and a risk he'll have to assume. He will come up the quarry road, leave the car, and approach the house from behind the barn. He'll attempt entrance from the patio area. I'd say a few minutes after sunset."

"To kill you?"

"I would imagine so."

Rocco looked deeply into his glass. "Makes sense. I'll get one of my men with your approximate build to wear some of your clothes and walk around the house with the lights on. We'll lay for the fink."

"I'd suggest some men in the barn with radio communications to the house, and another man near the wall switch that turns on the outside floods. When he passes the barn and is midway to the house, turn on the lights, and you have him from both directions."

"I'm with you. You and Bea had better stay in the cellar, where you'll be safe."

"Oh, no. Bea and I are going to be far away."

It was near eight when Lyon and Bea pulled into the parking lot of the Sound View Motel. The bright smile of the bellhop faded and his pace noticeably slowed as he approached the dusty pickup truck.

"Checking in, sir?" he asked.

"I called ahead for a reservation," Lyon said. He followed the bellhop to the registration desk with the sinking feeling that they'd request payment in advance, and he hoped Bea had enough with her to cover the room and dinner.

"Congratulations, Senator Wentworth." The manager's hand reached for Bea's and she smiled. "I saw your nomination on television this afternoon, and it's an honor to have the next secretary of the state at the Sound View."

"Thank you, Mr. —" She peered at the small red name tab on the manager's lapel. "—Mattaloni. Are you any relation to—"

"My cousin."

Lyon wasn't quite sure whether the suite with private terrace overlooking the ocean was the bridal or the presidential suite, but the complimentary bottle of sherry was excellent. As Bea showered, he sat on the terrace and flipped idly through the large menu, debating about calling down for room service.

"YOU KNOW, WENTWORTH," Bea shouted from the shower, "I really should be caucusing."

"I had something else in mind."

"Uh-huh. Maybe after."

"First, a magnificent steak with good wine in celebration."

Bea came out of the shower wearing a terry-cloth robe and toweling her hair as she moved behind him and kissed his neck. "You know, I still can't believe it."

"I'm very proud of you, Bea. You've been given a great honor."

She took the glass from his hand and sipped. "I meant your solving the murders."

"I'm sorry I brought the pickup to the convention hall. I couldn't find the keys to your car."

She laughed. "I didn't mind that, and the TV people thought it was funny. But what took you so long?"

"I went for a balloon ride."

"YOU WHAT? Never mind. I'm not going to ask why." She sat next to him as they watched the sun settle over the water. "No one in the world knows where we are. No reporters, no politicians, no Rainbows." She rolled the towel into a turban around her head. "What about the police captain in Breeland—what's his name?"

"Murdock. For a while I thought he was mixed up with Rainbow, but actually he's just overzealous. Rocco and Norbert are going to set up something next week."

"That sounds like entrapment."

"Bea, if you'd heard what Rocco told me, how the man hits people with complete disregard for their rights. . ."

"It's still entrapment, and I think . . . I think I'll change the subject for the time being. All that's happened was Danny Nemo's plan to con Dawkins for the money?"

"It was almost as if Dawkins had asked to be conned. He saw in what Danny was offering a method of control that could be used again and again."

"That's rather horrifying. But you knew it was Danny before the convention."

"I suspected, but we had to have the definite proof and the tie-in with Dawkins and the bank records. His reaction to seeing you was the final requirement."

"And the final clue. *Les jeux sont fait,* the play is made. Danny was the only suspect who was an inveterate gambler. 'The play is made,' the last thing said before the wheel is spun at Monte Carlo."

"Where Danny was last year."

"Exactly."

They ate on the terrace as the last vestige of summer light streaked the sky.

"For some reason motels make me feel wanton," Bea said softly.

"Things from your dark past that you haven't told me about?"

"Nope. Just being so alone together and—"

They both jumped as the phone rang.

"WENTWORTH, YOU TOLD ME NO ONE KNEW WE WERE HERE!"

"Well, just one," Lyon said as he picked up the phone. "Wentworth here."

"We got him, old buddy. Just like you said," Rocco roared exultantly over the phone. "A few minutes ago when it turned dark, between the house and the barn, gun in hand and a safe-deposit box key on a chain around his neck."

"Trouble?"

"We had him in a crossfire. He froze and dropped his gun without a whimper."

"Thanks, Rocco. Thanks for everything." Lyon clicked off the connection.

"It's over."

"Yes." The phone rang again, and he lifted the receiver with a movement of resignation. "Hello."

"It's your illustrious illustrator," Stacey's jubilant voice said on the other end of the line.

"One question, one small question. How in the hell did you find out where we were?"

"Somebody named Hocco or Locco answered your phone at home. I told him it was a matter of life and death, and that I had to talk to you."

"I think we've had enough of the life-and-death business for a while," Lyon said almost inaudibly. "What is it, Stacey?"

"Knew you'd want to know that Robin and I have been collaborating on the new book drawings. We've really got it, and we're catching a plane and will be up there in four hours with the preliminary sketches."

"Not tonight, Stacey."

"First thing in the morning."

"Day after tomorrow," Lyon said hopefully.

"We've got the motif for the whole book. I've got a hell of a talented kid here, Lyon. We're putting both our names down as artists."

"What about the Point?"

"Plenty of others for that. I've got a girl here who's an artist. How many do you find like that? Besides, I never was that happy in the military myself."

"In Korea, I sometimes felt that way."

"See you the day after tomorrow with the drawings. I'll pick up the manuscript then."

"It's not quite finished," Lyon replied. "But I'll get on it."

"Do that, Wentworth. You do that."

Lyon hung up, rang the switchboard to cut off further calls, and then turned to face Bea. "That was—"

"Stacey, and he's very excited."

"Exactly."

"Maybe you should work on the book tonight."

"That wasn't exactly what I had in mind."

"What did you have in mind?"

As he watched her stand in the doorway with a penumbra of waning light surrounding her, a montage of recent events shuttled before him. Bea on the green introducing Randy Llewyn as Junior Haney's carefully placed shots barely missed her. Bea standing by the kitchen window as high-velocity bullets shattered the glass inches from her head.

She gave him a hesitant smile and slowly opened her robe and let it fall to the floor. She was very alive, and he loved her.

"You still haven't said what you had in mind."

"I'll explain later," Lyon Wentworth said as he stepped toward his wife.